The Crabby Old Git Compilation

Volume 1

Phil Kingsman

Dedication

For Life's Cynics, Wherever You Are!

.

Table of Contents

Acknowledgements

Series proof-reader and copy editor: Maureen Vincent-Northam.

Cover layout created by Paul Finney:

—

1 The Crabby Old Git on Cruising

Dear Reg,

Cheers for the email you sent on Tuesday afternoon asking for my advice about cruising from a man's point of view. What you said in the pub on Tuesday night now makes sense.

It was unfortunate that the big bloke standing next to you at the bar thought you were making a pass at him – looking back, I suppose the fact that you had your hand on his shoulder in order to squeeze past him while you were talking to me about cruising for men, didn't help.

People are so intolerant these days and seem to take offence at the most innocent of comments. I thought him kneeing you in the plums was most uncalled for. When he poured my pint down the front of your trousers, it was his way of making amends by cooling the affected parts, don't you think?

While I'm on the subject, I know you felt I'd let you down in not remonstrating with the bruiser. However, I thought it was more important I rushed outside to see if, perchance, a police constable might be passing by - alas, as you know, no such luck.

Anyway, I'm sure your trousers have dried out by now and the smell of beer largely evaporated. Also, I'm sorry that the injury to your Crown Jewels has left you limping on both feet. All I would say is, don't be too self-conscious about it; men of character will simply assume that you're recovering from a vasectomy and that your advancing years make the feat all the more remarkable.

So, back to cruising. As you know, Maude and I are veterans and with all due modesty, I like to think I'm an expert on the subject. It's true that I'm not fond of water unless it's mixed with alcohol, but Maude believes undulating salt water beneath a 100,000 ton metal box to be both invigorating for our sex life and good for moving the bowels and I can tell you that my bowels move much more freely when I am afloat.

The first thing you need to understand is that booking a cruise is not as simple as it may at first appear. There are so many questions your wife requires you to answer – and it's important to remember that unless you are telepathic, each requires a response that is totally opposite to the logical side of your brain. Let me give you an example. If you were to ask me which part of the world might make for an interesting cruise, I might suggest the eastern Mediterranean, to which I'm sure you would say, "That's a great suggestion, thank you." Give that answer to a woman and she is likely to say, "So what's wrong with the Caribbean then?"

The trick here is to listen to any subtle hints your better half may deviously slip into conversations prior to booking. It's vitally important that you do not respond to these hints. Instead, store these titbits deep in your brain and spit them out with confidence when asked the destination question. With a bit of luck, you might convince her that great minds think alike.

Of course, it is far more likely she will inwardly digest that she has bested you again. In reality, who gives a shit as long as the damn boat has got a bar, doesn't leak and has a place to hide from the world when the mood takes you? In this respect, I like to think of it as a shed on water.

Of more importance is the grade of cabin you fork out for (strike that. For 'cabin' read 'stateroom' – just shows how stupid some people are in believing a box in which you couldn't swing a cat is some kind of baronial hall).

The crazy thing about cruise ships is that the higher the deck you book, the more you pay. Don't you think it's kind of stupid to pay more to be tossed around like a bottle cork in rough seas, rather than being tucked away in the cheaper little boxes, er, staterooms in the pit of the bloody ship?

And now we come to the greatest dilemma of all. Inside – or a room with a view, so to speak. Don't be fooled by those idiots who say it doesn't matter. Unless you're a bloody masochist (or fantasist who likes wearing fluffy pink handcuffs, leather underpants and a blindfold), being flung around like a pea in a mad referee's whistle is not my idea of fun (unlike the fluffy handcuffs bit – but don't tell Maude or she will be getting ideas I can well do without, what with my bowels and all).

Just make sure you can see the wet stuff when it takes your fancy by paying for a window – otherwise it won't be so much *Fifty Shades of Grey* in the bedroom, as fifty shades of crap down the toilet. Of course, if you really want to show off, there's always the option to go for a balcony cabin (sod it, a box in a boat is a cabin – a stateroom's in a mansion, end of). However, I just don't think it's worth it.

It's not as if you can use it to pee over the side if you get caught short during the night, since it's likely to be sucked back in through the air vents and sprayed all over unsuspecting lovey-dovey types strolling along the deck. Now you might say it would serve them right for still getting up to that sort of thing, but I like to think it's the more refined sort of person who cruises. Anyway, there's always the washbasin if needs must – just so long as the wife doesn't find out.

Reg, I'll need to email you back in a few minutes with the rest of my advice, since Maude is shouting me. For some reason she wants me to get the muck from under her feet, at least I think that's what she's saying, though why she wears slippers to mow the lawn is beyond me. Anyhow, speak to you soon.

***

Hi Reg,

Maude is feeling better now that she's got a couple of things off her chest, it seems there was nothing wrong with her slippers, and so what if I have to cook my own lunch. So, it's chicken-ding for me. Aren't microwaves a fantastic invention!

Now back to this cruising malarkey. When you arrive at the cruise terminal, in my experience it's best to adopt a 'yes dear' attitude. You will understand that the sight and sound of several hundred excited women is something that strikes fear into the hearts of all real men. Maude usually goes into assertive mode.

"Get the cases out of the car. Have you got change for the porter's tip? Don't forget to check that the cases have still got the luggage labels on them, where are the passports?"

And it gets worse; next the personal attacks begin.

"Fasten your jacket; you look like a sack of potatoes."

"I thought you'd cleaned your shoes? You really do look like something the cat's brought in."

Well, truth be told, I don't know about you but whatever I wear I look like a sack of potatoes. And as for cats, what the hell are they for anyway? In fact, as you will no doubt find out if you go ahead and book a cruise, the real reason for your tramp like appearance will be that she's run you ragged before you even left the house.

What with packing the car, feeding the fish, taking the dog to the kennels and pleading with the neighbour (who, if you're like me, you haven't spoken to for 12 months other than the occasional manly nod) to put your rubbish out for collection on the appointed day.

In my case I can hear you say that not talking to my neighbour was down to me. On this I totally disagree. Was it really my fault that his son, the dastardly Justin, lobbed his tennis ball onto my beautiful new barbeque from over the fence? And how was I to know that the stupid ball would explode just as the brat bent over the charcoal while I tried to retrieve the damn thing. I have to say that the mixture of soot, hickory chippings and chicken tikka all over his chops was a great improvement on things.

However, I do concede that adding a splash of tomato ketchup did cause his father to think the boy had burst an artery. In my defence, I already had the bottle in my hand and subconsciously squirted it as if to douse the smouldering poultice he had acquired.

Anyway, the real reason for all this angst from the wife will be that for many cruisers, the arrival hall will be the first opportunity they have to eye up the competition. You see many feel the need to confirm their place in the social pecking order at the earliest opportunity. Clothes, hand luggage, laptops, jewellery, speech pattern (vowels and volume) – all are of vital importance to the seasoned cruiser, and especially, Maude.

Another important sign of social standing is signalled by which queue you join. For ordinary folk, it's easy. You just look for the longest one and join it. For those special people (and they will be easy to spot due to the loud manner in which they enquire, "Which way to the express check-in?")

Such travellers also engage in Masonic like rituals. In particular, the judicious ruffling of their lapel badge whenever eyes fall upon them; the badge, you see, will denote the 'loyalty tier' that they have earned with the cruise line and, therefore, how much filthy lucre they apparently have (or the melted state of their credit cards). Nevertheless, appearances can be deceptive, and I have on more than one occasion tracked such couples (they usually are couples). You would be surprised at the number that book the cheapest possible cabins – since once you are in the public areas, who the hell knows what grade of cruise you have booked.

I have to admit to almost getting into trouble one time by being accused of stalking an elderly woman, but that's another story and anyway, Maude let me back into our own cabin after a couple of hours. Anyway, once you've had your passports checked, photograph taken, credit card swiped to make sure they have their hands on your loot before you put a foot on board, and cruise card issued, it will be onwards to the gangplank.

This is where you will first encounter the poor man's paparazzi. They will be waiting to mug you with their digital cameras and the dodgiest looking backdrop you will ever be photographed against. Take my advice, just smile but close your eyes for spite – and in any case, you don't have to buy the grotesque results (and for the price they charge you could hire a proper photographer).

It's at this point that you will be sorry if you stashed an overabundant supply of spirits in the hope of saving yourself a few bob in the bars. They won't mind too much if you have secreted the odd half bottle, but they get really touchy about bringing a mini brewery on board with you. Mean sods you might say, given you pay pub prices and they get to keep the equivalent of what you'd have paid in duty down at the Dog and Duck.

In the past, Maude has suggested I stick a couple of bottles down my trouser legs. Naturally I refused on the grounds that my body is a temple not to be tampered with by secretions of any sort. In any event, you know that I am a martyr to my varicose veins and have enough trouble putting one foot in front of the other, without being made to walk like someone who had been on the back of a horse for two weeks solid.

Once on the ship you will have a ringside view of what I like to call 'the great hustle'. Check out reception and the guys behind the desk looking harassed before the ship's propeller has turned a revolution. You can bet the demand for cabin upgrades has started.

"It's got an obstructed view."

"My wife's a light sleeper; we need to be away from the launderette."

"Last time we were on we got an upgrade, and we are good customers of yours."

It rarely works of course but there you have it, hell hath no fury like a cruise passenger on the make.

Okay so you're on board and your cabin won't be ready for an hour or so. What to do? If you're sensible, you find a quiet corner and have a kip. In reality the missus will drag you to the buffet for your first taste of a ship's biscuit. All I can say is be afraid, be very afraid. Buffets on cruise ships are not places for the fainthearted. I count amongst my own campaign wounds, bruised ribs, scratched hands inflamed elbows, to say nothing of my cowed ego at having received one too many of those withering glances that only women can propel toward a man.

Usually this is the result of having the temerity to select that particular slice of ham or boiled egg segment that, unbeknown to me, had the personal name of the fat woman to my left tattooed into it like a stick of Blackpool rock.

Now if you've any sense, in such circumstances, you will assume a submissive posture. Failure to do so can often bring a sharp jab to the rib cage. Not via a finger, slap or punch from the lady concerned you understand. No, the offending weapon will invariably be her décolletage as she nudges you roughly out of the way. God knows what some women put in their bras, but the tips can often resemble, and have the effect, of a bullet hitting its mark.

That said, if you're lucky, and succeeded in remembering everything your wife said she wanted for lunch, your only remaining obstacle is to find

a table that isn't occupied by passengers who have sp
like a praying mantis. They do this in order to preser'
seats, while they wait for the better halves that are st'
chicken curry, or else being assaulted (see my earlier

strides
can s

One last piece of advice in not getting too close '
years who are as overweight as a pork pie on steroid_
found wearing the most generous of 'sportswear' bottoms. It is the case
that when such people waddle down the ship's corridors, they fart
rhythmically as if their lower body exhalations are precisely synchronised to
each step they take.

By keeping a safe distance, it is possible to avoid the worst of any odour,
while thinking about a tune that might chime with the resonance and beat
that the farting before you dictates. However, be warned. If the said person
begins to reach to the rear of their trousers as if plucking underwear from
the crack of their secret place, stand well back. In all likelihood such
ferreting about, with less than nimble fingers, will be to seek confirmation
that the fart hasn't a part embedded within it.

While on the subject, you should also seek to avoid standing too close to
such people when queuing, especially for food since the result is highly
likely to put you off your lunch. I speak of course, for those situations
where the substantial passenger in front of you drops their fork or some
other such thing and bends over to retrieve the said article.

Again, stand well back, since the act of bending forward will, sure as
eggs is eggs (and which will most certainly have the same noxious aroma),
result in a projectile fart being launched in your direction with laser like
accuracy. The danger here is that you do not acknowledge were the gaseous
substance has emanated from, meaning you get the blame from other
passengers who, though affected to a lesser extent due to their position in
the queue, will nonetheless seek to blame the person nearest them.

Anyway, sooner or later you will hear the 'bing bong' of the tannoy
system announcing that cabins are ready for occupation. This will be the
signal for the buffet to empty more quickly than shouting that the last
person in the room buys the beers.

Now if you have taken my advice and booked a cabin with a window,
once you manage to work out how to open the door with your cruise card,
you should be pleasantly surprised that you're able to take more than two

ithout cracking your forehead on the opposite end of the cabin and ee daylight.

If you can't see daylight, step back out of the wardrobe, ignore your wife's searing glare and head for the section of clear glass that should be in front of you. In such situations I find it best to rattle the coat hangers as if it were an intentional act by way of ensuring sufficient number are available and make no admission of guilt. Oh, and by the way, don't think that you're hearing voices in your head; it will just be the ship's TV on a continuous loop telling you how to abandon ship in the event that it hits an iceberg or some other such obstacle.

...A word of caution about the toilet, Reg.

Don't go looking for a chain to pull or a handle to press. You'll find a button to push on the wall. When you've done your 'business', the idea is to put the lid down (I know this is something intelligent men such as us find of little value. Does Judith complain as much as Maude moans at me about you leaving the lid up? Mars and Venus eh, Mars and Venus).

Anyway, on board you won't have any choice about the matter, if you are to dispatch your little gifts to the mother of all compactors, you'll have to put the lid down to hit the bloody button. Whatever you do, don't try to be inventive and make the mistake of reaching behind you while you're still sat on the throne. I can tell you from personal experience, it will feel like your meat and two veg. are being torn from your body like Guy Fawkes's legs on the rack in the Tower of London.

It took me some time to recover, let me tell you, and given your recent experience of being hammered in the plums, I would have thought the last thing you'd be looking for is to have your manhood stretched to within an inch of its life. I know women say that size doesn't matter, and I know there's not a man on this earth that believes that for a second, but better your little fella stays true to itself, rather than a few inches longer but good for nothing more than as a strop for that cutthroat razor I know you still use.

Now, if you're anything like me, the best thing you can do while Judith unpacks the suitcases is to have a quick kip so you stay out of trouble. Don't worry, you won't miss much and in any event the noise of the ship's engines, and the captain prattling over the intercom telling you the sail away party is about to begin will soon rouse you.

If you don't get up on deck sharpish, you stand little chance of getting near the port side of the ship (top tip, that's the left side looking toward the pointy bit of the boat), since the more seasoned cruisers will have shot to their favoured spot like a rat up a drainpipe. I'm afraid the days of listening to a military band playing *We Are Sailing* are long gone – there's not even piped music to be had these days. However, passengers seem to be drawn by some primeval urge to the sight of the dockside as it recedes, and to wave their hands whether there's anybody waving back at them or not.

Perhaps it's a feeling that they may never get to see dry land again. After all, rather like flying, there is nothing natural about leaving terra firma and trusting your soul to a metal box an inch or so thick. And think about it, you just paid several thousand pounds for the privilege. Stupid or what?

Time to be on your guard by the way; no sooner has the non-existent band stopped playing and churning water opens up between you and the dockside, than an army of waiters will be upon you pressing the *cocktail of the day, champagne* or some other concoction into your hand. Take note that this will not be without cost and the process of whisking your cruise card away from you to charge your account will have begun.

If you can't wait to spend money, then fine. If you've any sense, you'll wait 'till the bar opens and make friends with the staff. For as you know, no greater love hath man than for his trusty bartender.

In any event, shortly after leaving port, your first opportunity to witness entertainment on a grand scale will present itself to you. I speak, of course, of the renowned 'don't put your lifejacket on yet' ceremony.

To get a front seat row at the ceremony, you'll need to get back to your cabin and wait for the seven rings you will hear over the ship's tannoy. Normally such a signal would mean you need to leg it to the side of the ship and jump into a lifeboat pronto – sod that women and children first malarkey.

This time, (unless you're *very* unlucky) it will be to summon you to your muster station (which has nothing to do with salad dressing by the way) with your lifejacket in tow for a safety drill. If you've any sense you will hide away at the back of the room and volunteer for nothing.

Eventually the hubbub will subside and a rather jolly (sometimes hyper) member of the ship's company will bring the babbling mass to order. He or she will then introduce other members of the ship's company who will appear from amongst the throng as if by magic and take on the appearance of a shop mannequin.

And so, the entertainment begins. No sooner has the leader of the pack begun demonstrating how to fit their lifejacket than at least 10% of those assembled will begin, as if compelled by some secret signal, to don their own lifejackets. It will not matter how often, or how assertively the demonstrator pleads with people not to fit their lifejackets until the demonstration is complete.

This is, of course, an intentional action by the miscreants involved. It is, you see, a visual representation of the apparent superiority of the seasoned cruiser. It is important for them that those new to cruising should know their place and make homage to those who are more experienced in such matters.

The irony is that given the average age of cruisers, folk who have enough filthy lucre to be able to afford cruise after cruise are, to put it delicately, on the Grim Reaper's Christmas card list, living off a public-sector pension or from ill-gotten gains.

Either way, they are about as agile as a sloth and as sharp as a tin full of not very sharp things. This makes for a great deal of huffing and puffing, stifled shrieks of pain and quiet cursing from those in the immediate vicinity of these exhibitionists, as they fend off flying elbows, unsteady bodies and lifebelts on the run from their irascible owners.

Of course, the best is yet to come. Once the demonstration is completed, your hapless instructor will tell everyone to have a go at fitting their lifejacket. Picture the scene if you will, Reg. Two hundred people having left every ounce of common sense at the quayside, squashed into a room designed for a couple of dozen serious drinkers, suddenly transformed into the most stupid flock of sheep you've ever set your eyes on.

After a nanosecond of silence and furtive eyes checking out who is brave enough to make the first move, everyone follows whatever he or she does. I tell you, Reg, you just would not believe how many different ways human beings can invent to strap a bright orange bag filled with polystyrene onto their chest.

I say chest in the loosest possible way, since I've seen the darn things perched on top of people's heads and between their legs, the latter looking like some grotesque form of hernia support.

Oh, by the way, at this point don't delude yourself that the ship stabilisers are keeping the boat as steady as a rock while passengers get their sea legs. You'll still be in inshore waters and the briny will be like a millpond. You'll know when you're in open water, believe me, you'll know.

For goodness sake can a man have no peace? Reg, I'll need to email you back. Maude is calling me by my surname, so I've obviously done something wrong. To paraphrase a famous British explorer: I'm going now; I may be some time.

***

Hi Reg,

It's me again. If I live to be 100 I swear I'll never understand women. This morning, Maude asked me to nip into the village and get some concentrated fabric softener. I know this is what she asked me to get because she was standing by the washing machine at the time loading a week's worth of my underpants and favourite onesies.

Unfortunately, it seems I picked up a bottle of exterior drain cleaner by mistake. You know the problem, Reg, all those sodding bottles look the same on the shelf, and I really thought I was being a good husband when I got back, put the stupid stuff into the machine and set it going.

So, I really don't know what all the fuss is about. A dozen pairs of underpants and a couple of woolly onesies can't be that expensive to replace, can they? And anyway, Maude's been after a new washing machine for months now. It's a win-win situation as far as I'm concerned; Maude gets a new washing machine and I get underpants with proper elastic in them.

What I'm not going to get, it seems, is my dinner. Bugger.

Anyway, back to cruising. After the trauma of lifejacket training, it'll be time to head back to your cabin and get ready for the delights of dinner. Depending on which 'sitting' you've chosen, it'll now be a case of a fast shave and throwing a clean shirt on if you're on first-sitting or chilling out in preparation for second sitting.

One advantage of first sitting is that you get two chances to see whatever show is on that night, since they repeat twice nightly, so to speak. However, the poor sods on second sitting won't take kindly to you nicking the seats in the theatre – but I'll say more on that later.

A disadvantage of first sitting is that you have to rush around like a blue arse fly in the early evening to get ready in time and put up with hordes of screaming kids. Of course, you two will be cruise virgins and so you need to be wary of the pitfalls and protocols of the most stressful meal you will ever have had. As you enter the restaurant you will see the first of many examples of how stupid people can be when it comes to avoiding Montezuma's revenge, or as you and I may say down the Dog and Duck, 'the shits'.

We've all heard the tales of the dreaded norovirus. It really is worth noting this has got nothing to do with computers and has got everything to do with your bowels. It's a simple fact that if you put thousands of people in a tin can and some can't be bothered to wash their hands when they pointed Percy at the porcelain (and whatever the equivalent is for the gentler sex) you're going to get trouble.

In trying to prevent their darling passengers from experiencing the delights of crapping themselves and projectile vomiting at the same time (it's quite an art for anyone to get both sets of fluids into a receptacle at the same time, you know), your hosts will have thoughtfully placed hand sanitizers at the entrance to every restaurant and other eatery.

It beggars belief the number of people who actively go out of their way to avoid these little machines. Others will feign an attempt to use the thing by putting their hands into the dispenser, but pulling them out double quick, before the helpful gel can touch their skin.

It's no wonder they don't put peanuts on bars anymore and you wouldn't believe the contortions people go to in trying to open toilet doors without touching the handle. I've seen blokes stand in front of the door willing it to open as if by telepathy, then collecting a bloody nose by loitering too close as a bloke on the outside flings the thing open with the toe of his shoe to gain entry (since he doesn't want to touch the *outside* handle). Not a pretty sight. So, avoid what I call the norovirus pirates like the plague – unless you want to catch the plague, of course.

Once you settle at your table the fun really begins. With luck, the two of you will arrive first. This gives you the advantage of being a sitting tenant, making all that follow greet you as if you own the bloody thing. It's now that the 'sniffing' begins. What do I mean? Well, force a group of people together and several things begin to happen as if preordained:

1.   The women check out what the other women are wearing – and if they are coordinated

2.   Each person makes an instant judgement as to whether they like or dislike the other individuals

3.   Each table guest pigeonholes everyone else as to where they consider they fit on the social scale

All of this is happening while each grins pleasantly at the other. The crazy thing is, everyone knows what game is being played out, but it's impossible not to play.

...And now for the ultimate pigeon-holer. I'm willing to bet you a pint of best bitter that it won't be more than 5 minutes before somebody on your table asks you the immortal question:

"How many cruises have you been on?"

Don't be fooled. This has got absolutely nothing to do with any fetish for holidays you might have and everything to do with gathering evidence of your financial status. When you respond by saying 'this is our first time', your Inquisitor will respond by saying 'well this is a lovely ship and I'm sure you will enjoy it'.

What they actually want is for you to reciprocate by asking them how many times they have cruised before. Mark my words, this is the cue they have been waiting for and will regale you, often in excruciating detail, of the number of cruises they've had and on what ships they sailed (yawn, yawn).

Financial and social superiority established they will move onto their next victim. If you're very unlucky, you'll have a ship's officer hosting your table. Why unlucky you say? Well, in my experience, they will be bored to death and waiting with trepidation for the usual questions to be asked like:

"Do the crew stay on board overnight?" and...

"Do ships sink very often?" (I would have thought only once).

Above all, they will be wondering to themselves what the hell they've done to upset the captain that such punishment should have been meted out to them.

On the other hand, being on a hosted table can have some advantages. The officer will often treat his or her guests to the bottle of wine. And don't be fooled by this apparent generosity by reciprocating the gesture, since the officer will most definitely not be reaching into his or her own pocket. Instead you will be a beneficiary of the entertainment budget given to him for just such an event. So, just accept and drink!

If you're very unlucky you might be landed with a different officer every night (this may especially be the case if there are a number of young officers on board who are being made to cut their teeth with passengers).

In order to overcome their shyness, and palpable fear, they will have the same stock questions ready to be fired at you (including the one about if you've cruised before). This forces you and your table companions to trot out the same back story night after night after night.

What can be entertaining here is that as each evening unfolds, everyone's back story becomes more and more elaborate. I've yet to decide whether this is to overcome the boredom of having to repeat yourself, or an opportunistic attempt to improve their social standing amongst fellow guests by including details (real or imagined) that may have been omitted the previous evening. It can be enough to make you want to lose the will to live, or at least, get drunk.

One last thing on your dining companions, beware the guy (and it's always a bloke) who thinks it's his life mission to organise the rest of you. Maude and I went on a cruise a couple of years ago and as usual, sat next to each other for our evening meal (as did the other couples). However, the pompous arse sitting opposite me decided it would be good fun to mix everybody up in the name of social intercourse. Having floated the idea during the meal and taking no notice of everybody ignoring him, we came down to dinner the next evening to find little place setting cards telling us where we should sit.

Luckily the rest of the table arrived before the pompous sod and his long-suffering wife and totally ignored his pre-planning. I know it's childish, but it was a wonderful experience watching him sulk for the rest of the meal. Those little cards did not make another appearance.

Oh, I almost forgot, by the end of the meal you may realise that something else has happened, the ship will have started to move. By now you'll be into open water and at the mercy of the ocean currents. With a bit of luck of course it will be a gentle roll fit to put a baby to sleep.

However, my own experience is that it took three different cruises to finish the Beef Wellington I ordered. On each cruise the briny decided to make its presence known and the only Wellington I wished for was the rubber type that I could vomit into. Now, the slightest sight of that bloody dish sends me into a rapid decline.

On the subject of puke, I'll have more to say on the important subject of seasickness a little later in my email.

One other phenomenon you will become aware of from the first evening of your cruise, is that very many diners will accelerate their mastication (not to be confused with more deviant behaviour, Reg) as the courses progress. Why so, you may ask?

Well, as I shall cover in the next section of my little note to you, you will have realised that to stand any chance of getting a good seat in the theatre you'll need to throw your last course and coffee down your neck at a rate of knots – do forgive the pun. It's interesting to observe just how quickly some folk who, at all other times hobble around the ship, can suddenly turn into athletes of Olympian standard when it comes to getting a front row seat.

Be especially wary of those with Zimmer frames and other walking accoutrement. Aluminium may be regarded as a light alloy, but when it's attached to someone well into the third age hurtling to the theatre, the damage it can do to one's shins is not to be underestimated.

Hang on, Reg, somebody at the door. I'll get back to you shortly.

***

Morning, Reg, sorry about that.

Yet another bloody double-glazing salesman who rang the bell on our double-glazed porch, then rattled the letterbox of our double-glazed door to ask me if we wanted any double glazing fitted. When I asked him whether it looks like we needed any double glazing, he took a step back, scanned his eyes over the forest of double glazing in front of him and said,

"Have you ever thought of replacing your double glazing with beautiful hardwood frames, we do a wonderful range you know."

Now you know I'm a man of impeccable temperament, Reg. But it took all of my considerable willpower not to shove the leaflets he was holding somewhere that doesn't often see the light of day.

Nevertheless, you would have been proud of me and instead, I pointed to the 'no hawkers, beggars, or especially double -glazing salesmen' laminated sign on the side window of the porch. In what I thought was a nice gesture, he waited until he was at the end of the drive before turning to me and raising two fingers.

For a man of his young years, I thought it was rather touching that, as a nod of respect to me, he was demonstrating his understanding of English history in mimicking Mr Churchill's famous gesture.

I thought it only appropriate that I returned the gesture. He shouted something I couldn't quite catch, which I am sure would have been a credit to his generation. Okay, let's assume you've made it into the theatre to sample the night's entertainment. If you don't get there pronto, you will then experience two types of behaviour exclusive to human beings.

1.   There are the couples who, despite choosing an empty row of seating, determine to occupy the two end seats at the end of the row, forcing everybody else to clamber over their (usually) ample thighs.

2.   Women (men have rarely the bottle) who take one seat, then disperse any form of clothing, chattel or other inanimate object across adjacent seats. Not only that, such people are to be seen standing to their tallest extent glaring at the theatre entrances with an exaggerated stair, waving furiously with both hands as if up to their neck in water trying to beckon a reluctant lifeboat.

Woe betides any man who dare disturb any of the aforementioned chattels at peril of damage to their physical and/or emotional wellbeing.

Anyway, once you do manage to get a seat, you've got the entertainment to look forward to. This will include the ship's Theatre Company, who I must say for the most part are excellent artists.

Their act can be particularly riveting to watch when the ship is rolling. I have to admire their skill, and bravery, at slinging their legs in the air and belting a song out, even as they're sliding from one side of the stage to the other while still smiling manically.

The other type of act you are bound to see, the 'headline' comic, can use this to his or her advantage. Given that most of them will be tanked up with libation well before they set foot on stage, they are able to disguise any frailty of posture by rolling with the ship.

The people I do feel sorry for, however, are the musicians. As you know, Reg, I was an accomplished trumpet player in my youth, so I know what it's like to get a fat lip from a stainless-steel mouthpiece rattling into your gob.

Anyway, back to the comic. You'll know you're in for a car crash when the compare introduces him (it's always a man) and during his build up uses the phrase 'star of TV and radio'. Pound to a pinch of salt this will mean the comic's last appearance was on black and white TV or valve radio.

Just one other thing, Reg. Don't sit in the front row under any circumstances. You can bet your life that the worse the comic's act is going, in desperation, the more he will try to involve his audience – and that means roping in anyone in the front row who is daft enough to give him eye contact.

Given his jokes and other shenanigans will be crap anyway, the last thing you want is to be tarred by association. Not to be satisfied with inflicting 40-year-old jokes on his captive audience, at the end of his act he will be off the stage like greased lightning. Now the audience might think he's just keen to get back to the bar to console himself. In fact, he will be waiting to ambush you in the theatre foyer, where he will use all his guile to flog you his autobiography.

You'd be amazed just how many people are suckered into buying a book they don't want, signed by a bloke they don't know. Ah well, there's always the local charity shop you can offload it on once you get home.

Just a word about seasickness, Reg, since I've been talking about the ship rolling over the last couple of minutes. Now I'm not going to be one of those people who seem to delight in spreading scare stories about pitching boats and vomiting passengers. No, that's not my style, and I take no pleasure in talking about such things. However, there are one or two things you should know. The first thing is that no matter how big the bloody boat is, it's going to move.

Yes, they all have stabilisers, but if you think back to that bike that your Graham had when he was a little 'un. You may remember that his stabilisers certainly stopped him from falling off (at least after that unfortunate incident of you using the wrong size bolts that resulted in him being catapulted into those nettles. He still reckons he's got the scars from that you know). But it didn't stop him rocking from side to side when he was riding, did it?

Well, ship stabilisers are the same (and I'll swear they don't put them out all the time in rough weather to save money on diesel – they just tell you they have been deployed and hope for a placebo effect). Now you might be one of the lucky buggers that don't suffer from sea sickness – just like Maude. I, on the other hand, am a martyr to regurgitating carrot (why *does* vomit always look like carrots and smell like dead rats?). This demonstrates to you just what lengths I am prepared to go to keep my better half satisfied (it beats the alternative).

If you've never had seasickness before let me give you a tip about the warning signs.

There aren't any warning signs.

The best piece of advice I can give you is that if you do come over all funny (and assuming you're not having a stroke or suchlike), is for you to head down to reception. This is always set low and at the centre of the ship (this is good planning since it negates the need for passengers to use a rope and crampons when using the gangplank). The disadvantage is that there are no windows in reception since it makes for keeping the water out that bit easier.

So, while the motion will be less in the reception area, you won't be able to see what's going on outside and won't have any warning as the foaming seas get ready to lob you from one side of reception to the other. One of the most irritating features of bad weather is that the captain insists on keeping passengers updated over the tannoy system. Now ship's captains, rather like airline pilots, are specially trained in that peculiar way of speaking which sounds like they are stroking a cat.

It doesn't matter how bad things are, you bet the captain will tell you how very pleased he is with the way the ship is coping with the force ten gale that's chucking you, and everybody else, around the bloody thing like a rag doll.

I remember one trip in particular where the weather was so bad that the captain ordered all doors leading to the decks to be locked, and in the bars on the highest decks to be closed. I can tell you that there wasn't much food served that day, and what was served ended up being physically recycled over the carpets.

Maude insisted that we should go to the buffet because, she said, we would get a better view of the sea (do you now understand what I have to put up with?) Something you need to understand about most buffet areas is that they have tiled floors. While this is hygienic and advantageous for quickly cleaning up bodily fluids, it is a distinct disadvantage when the ship is rolling like a rubber duck in a bathtub.

Never had I experienced such a cacophony of noise as crockery and cutlery flew from assorted shelves and drawers. The site of passengers clinging grimly to their wicker chairs sliding to left, then right (I should say port and starboard I suppose) was enough to give even the most reckless souls the heebie-jeebies.

So here is my top tip. It's the captain's job to keep people calm and reassured, so don't take any notice of him. When you see new sick bags being placed upside down between the hand rails and walls by the crew, know that you need to take precautionary action.

My best advice is that once you start feeling as though you are having an out of body experience, brought back to reality through the physical sensation of the contents of your stomach leaching out of your ears, then heed these words of advice:

Open your wallet and pay for a jab in the arse.

I can say with absolute confidence that having a little prick in your bottom is much more effective than all the pills you can swallow. Disregard also all those seasoned cruisers who proffer their sage advice for remedies such as:

1. *Eat as much food as you can to keep a lining on your stomach*: This is a contradiction in terms and is bound to end in misery, flatulence and a crap-fest

2. ***Keep your eyes on the horizon:*** Who the feck wants to stare like a man possessed at an imaginary line in the distance for hours on end, while holding onto feboat davit as if it was your mother and being yanked from pillar to post and soaked to the skin by Neptune's spittle

3. ***Wear an acupuncture pressure band.*** This is for Hippies and other tree-huggers and in my experience gives no relief other making your wrist itch (which, I suppose, *is* a form if distraction)

4. ***Wear a copper bracelet***: All this will do for you is to turn your wrist Day-Glo green, and set you up as a lightning rod for the bolts of rabid electricity from the sky that your natty bangle will have invited (at least the smell of singed hair and flaming eyebrows will take your mind off the overwhelming urge to vomit)

Now you know I'm no fan of hypodermic needles, and before you remind me, yes, I do recall being indirectly responsible for that pretty young nurse falling into a state of unconsciousness. But as you will well recall, it was her third attempt to draw that blood sample.

In restraining my arm's natural inclination to resist penetration by sharp object, she bore at least some of the responsibility for that metal kidney dish hitting her between the eyes and the recoil that resulted in her bouncing off the haemorrhoid cushion on that commode before hitting the drugs cabinet.

In any event all's well that ends well, as they say. As you know, my blood results were completely normal. Anyway, flying nurses aside, you will not regret spending the dosh to keep the contents of your stomach where they rightly belong.

My own experience should provide you with all the reassurance that you need. Having made the mistake of booking an inside cabin some years ago and being woken up by the rhythmic thumping of the ship's bow striking a very angry sea, I thought that the end of the world was nigh.

My humour was not helped by the note left by Maude, informing me she had gone on deck to take in what she described as, "All those lovely waves." After half an hour of scurrying to and from the bathroom with its floor getting slippier by the minute, I resolved to ring the medical centre and speak almost coherently to request a jab.

I have to say I remember very little else. It being an inside cabin with the lights turned off, my world was in complete darkness. What I do faintly recall is the door opening, the cotton sheet I was hiding under being removed, a voice asking my name and age, then 'wallop', needle in buttocks.

My, "I couldn't give a shit, I want to die please," reaction was stilled by a voice from the gods saying, "You'll sleep for the rest of the day, and don't drink alcohol for 24 hours."

I gave thanks for the first instruction and thought 'bollocks' to the latter. Nevertheless, the little prick did its job even if Maude did give me a hard time for, as she put it, "Lazing about for the day."

Just a minute, Reg. The telephone's ringing and since Maude has gone gallivanting to the shops for food and such like, I'll need to get it. I'll email you back in a couple of minutes.

**

Hi Reg,

It was one of those sodding telephone calls telling me I was entitled to claim for miss-sold loan payment protection insurance. As you know, Reg. Maude's mantra is that if we can't afford it, we don't buy it, so as I said to the poor sod following a script on the other end of the line, we have never had a loan, so no claim can be possible.

Nevertheless, the bored young man continued by insisting they used a sophisticated customer database to pinpoint those individuals who were eligible to claim. When I challenged him on the accuracy of said database, he assured me he had the details in front of him but could not reveal the contents due to data protection legislation (given the details were supposed to be about me, that seemed a bit of a contradiction, don't you think?)

Anyway, when he finally realised he wasn't going to get anywhere, he asked me if I knew anybody else that would like to claim; so much for their sophisticated customer database.

One of the more fascinating aspects of cruising is what are called 'sea days'. As the name implies, these refer to those periods when the ship is travelling between ports of call. During such times the day takes on a familiar routine.

After the usual bun fight at the buffet, or Groundhog Day breakfast in the restaurant, you will be subjected to a blistering variety of activities, which you will do well to avoid. My personal preference is to find a quiet corner in my favourite bar and keep well away from those individuals who feel compelled to be organised by somebody else during their every waking hour.

Why on earth people feel the need to learn needlecraft, how to decorate a cake, how to fold napkins or learn the foxtrot is beyond me. And let's not go near the subject of bingo, whist drives or 'complete the jigsaw in the library' activity. One distraction in particular should be avoided by all sensible men. I speak of course, of the dreaded 'shop sale'. I ask you, Reg, how can it be that goods being sold at full price on the first day of your cruise are miraculously on sale at 20% off two days later?

In any event it always has the desired effect amongst the ladies. I have lived long enough to know that a man must never physically come between a woman (or worse, a posse) striding belligerently forward as she zeros into the object of her desire (and I don't mean a bloke).

I tell you, Reg, such ladies give no quarter to either men or each other. It really is a case of "It's mine, bitch, out of my way." It's at such times that men of even the strongest disposition cower in fear and seek out other male company so that they may heal their mental scars and stroke each other's egos.

Well, Reg, it's time to talk about that other ordeal that you must surely endure. I speak of course of the dreaded organised tour (or as I like to call them, sore feet and empty wallet events).

Stay well out of any attempt to select any of these tours on behalf of your wife. This, my friend, is firmly woman territory. Your only role is to surrender all control of your cash.

Worse, you will be made to sit through interminable presentations known as 'Port Lectures', during which you will endure a 45-minute sales pitch and death by PowerPoint slide. Such events are made all the more nauseating (in a truly physical sense) by the gentle rolling of the ship.

This makes the projector shake, the effect of which is magnified on screen causing you to question if you are having an attack of vertigo, or as my mother used to say, some other 'funny do'.

In any event all this pales into insignificance when compared to the tour itself. Having been made to get up at the crack of dawn and to force breakfast down your throat at a time that one should still be dreaming of more pleasurable diversions, you will then be herded down the gangplank like cattle on a day out from which they are destined not to return.

Tour ticket in hand (or should I say, your wife's hand), you will be led to a neat line of waiting coaches. However, before you get anywhere near your transport, the ship's paparazzi will once again seek to capture your image.

It won't be enough that they trapped you before you joined the ship, when you were eating, while you were sleeping, when you were picking your nose and every other 'photo opportunity' they can think of.

Anyway, when you've said "no" for the tenth time, you can now make a dash for the coach. Don't expect to get the front seats, these are always miraculously taken by the old bird and her husband who are usually to be seen doddering about the ship.

The look of satisfaction in their eyes as they stare you out when you shuffle past them leads me to believe that favours are being called in. It's at this point I often shiver as my mind processes a mental picture of physical contact that doesn't bear exploring.

For the rest of the morning I can guarantee you will spend your time thinking why you paid a king's ransom to fall asleep on the coach, be corralled off the vehicle at 30-minute intervals for a 15-minute tour of yet another church, whose history is explained to you by a man in a straw hat and broken umbrella, and who walks at the pace of a thoroughbred greyhound chasing the first rabbit it's seen in weeks.

To add insult to injury, most passengers will begin to get very restless as midday approaches. You see, even though they paid an arm and half a leg to join the tour, they will make sure they are transported back to the ship in time for yet another bun fight at the buffet.

And so, Reg, just as eggs are eggs, the end of your cruise will come around all too soon (or if the weather's been bad, the norovirus mugged you, or you got sick to death of eating, not soon enough.), which leads me to advise you on the last day on board.

You will notice a subtle change in the mood of the ship. While your fellow passengers will become quieter, more reflective and revert to type, the officers and crew will seem to have a certain lightness of foot and readiness to share a joke (I take this as a sign of relief that they get rid of the lot of you – though they also know it won't take long for the passengers on the next cruise to be just the same as the current lot).

Of course, any levity on the part of the crew diminishes rapidly as the evening wears on, since they know what lies ahead of them in the hours to come. I mean of course, getting shot of several thousand pieces of luggage, putting up with the gripes of depressed passengers and steeling themselves for reloading enough luggage to clothe the developing world, then hearing the same old hustles for cabin upgrades.

One last ritual to go through will be played out over dinner. Since by then you will have packed your suitcases (I use the term 'you' in the loosest possible sense, of course), you will all be in your scruff and in reflective mood.

Nevertheless, each of your table companions will be doing their best to tell you how much they've enjoyed the cruise, if only to convince themselves that the vast amount of money they spent on their cabin, cappuccinos and assorted memorabilia emblazoned with the cruise line's logo, really was value for money.

It's now that many of you will say to each other, "We must keep in touch, do pop in if ever you're in the area." Naturally, it will be incredibly difficult since each couple will purposely fail to hand over their address or contact details. Handshakes proffered and air kisses completed, your table companions will revert to absolute strangers the second that they are out of your sight, and you can return to your cabin in the sure knowledge that anything not screwed down, will have been removed by your steward to make sure you don't filch it as a memento of your holiday and reminder of your empty wallet.

Having placed all luggage outside your cabin, save for the shoulder bag containing a toothbrush, shaver and your wife's face cream in case of kidnap, it will be time to retire to bed. A few hours later, and certainly if you've not showed your face to the steward by 8am he will show his face to you, you will be sitting on your bed wondering where the previous fortnight had gone and whether the withered state of your finances was really worth it.

However, before you have time to ponder this question, your cabin steward will be reminding you that you will need to vacate by 9 o'clock sharp. Gone is all pretence that this was a holiday, and since the tip he will get from you is, these days, automatically added to your on board account, the cynic may argue that he has little to gain from encouraging you to hang around. After all, he's got the room to strip and the TV to turn on to tell people what to do when the ship is sinking.

On your last morning you will not have the option of taking breakfast in the restaurant, which will be closed. Instead, you guessed it, time for the last bun fight at the O.K. Corral. If you take my advice, you will leave the selection and delivery of your breakfast to your wife. By now all men, even the brave ones, will have been beaten into submission by the women with pointy bras and loose bowels, so it will be time for the sisters to fight it out for themselves. The final act will be to huddle in your appointed 'muster station' and await the call to disembark. Don't expect any semblance of good manners or courtesy in this room as you joust for a seat with your once compatriot cruisers.

Anyway, in the fullness of time (and it can seem a *long* time), you'll find yourself being ushered towards the gangplank with undue haste and the absence of the friendly ceremony with which you were greeted, just those few short days ago. ...And now just one last challenge before heading home to the delight and sanctuary of your shed. It's time to find your suitcases in the serried ranks of assorted bags that seem to disappear into the far distance of the arrivals hall. My advice is to have the foresight to have kept back especially for disembarkation, a pair of trousers made of the thickest material possible. This should be complemented by a pair of long socks, again made of thick material, topped (or should I say bottomed) with a stout pair of shoes.

No, I'm not suggesting you stop off for a spot of hill walking on the way home; instead this will be preparation for withstanding depressed ex-passengers venting their anger at re-joining the human race, by steering their baggage trolley like a demon possessed. Having finally retrieved your suitcases and successfully fought off the mad sod (there's always one) who insists you've stolen one of his suitcases, it will be time to head for the taxi, whose driver will try to fleece you, since he assumes everybody who takes a cruise is made of money and don't know their way to the train station, or wherever.

After this final episode of aggravation, and before you can settle in to the transport that will deliver you back to normality, you will ask yourself this question.

"Was it worth it and would I do it again."

To which your wife will answer,

"Next summer we're going to the Caribbean."

Although I do not recommend showing any sign of enthusiasm, if you're like me you'll have a quiet smile to yourself while thinking…

'The Caribbean…sounds good'.

END

2 The Crabby Old Git on Exercise

Dear Reg

I thought I would drop you a line to tell you about Maude's latest fad. She has taken it into her head that we (she means me) are unfit and in need of exercise. No ordinary exercise you understand, but the organised kind where you have to pay to be humiliated and driven to exhaustion. And the worst thing about this is that it has nothing to do with a trip to Amsterdam, red lights, leather thongs or a cat 'o nine tails.

Anyway, before I tell you any more about her tawdry plan to stretch things of mine that she has no right touching (wedding vows notwithstanding), how are you and is your black eye looking any better yet? It beggars belief that old woman could have misunderstood what you said to her at the bread counter. From what you told me, all you said in all innocence was that you were looking for "those naughty baguettes". I simply do not see how she could have interpreted this as you, accusing her of being a "haughty fat git".

In any event, I see no justification for her clouting you in the eye with the very baguette you were seeking to purchase. As a mature and sensible man, I think your action in running away was entirely justified, and I think that the supermarket manager's rugby tackle on you was a little over the top, to say the least. And to make matters worse, from what you've told me, despite having your apologies accepted (even if grudgingly) you were escorted off the premises without your baguette.

However, a word of advice, Reg. I think it's time you took those sunglasses off. From what I hear (and you know I am not one for tittle tattle), they are doing nothing for your reputation around the village. What with the cold weather and all, the combination of sunglasses and that long brown raincoat (which I know is your favourite) is feeding the warped imagination amongst those of a lesser intellect that you are a pervert.

I want you to know that you can still rely on my friendship; I should just say though, if we are to meet in the Dog and Duck as planned tonight, it might be better if you wear an eye patch and that dapper little bomber jacket Judith got you for Christmas. Anyway, back to this exercise malarkey, which, as you know, Reg, is a subject on which I am something of an expert.

Maude's obsession started a few days ago when some callow youth delivered a leaflet from the local sports and leisure centre (a contradiction in terms if ever I've heard one). I say deliver in the loosest possible sense, since the lad was clearly inexperienced and in need of training in customer service.

At the time, I was busy using my new turbo power washer to clean an Alpine resort quantity of bird crap off the divide which stands between civilisation and what I loosely call, my neighbour. As you know, Reg, I have on more than one occasion suggested to the fool over the fence that he should desist from encouraging enough birds to fill the cast of an Alfred Hitchcock film from swarming into his back garden.

Given their stupid cat, he should know better than anybody that no bird with an ounce of care for its own survival would set claw on grass – or mud to be more precise.

Instead they perch on my bloody fence with one eye on the cat and the other on his wonky table, which is always weighed down with seed in quantities sufficient to feed the world's entire population of tits for a month.

So, out of frustration at seeing food they cannot touch (or peck, so to speak), the feathered morons crap all over my fence – and if that isn't bad enough the cat, which is also frustrated because it can't get at the birds, relieves its irritation by crapping all over my bloody begonias, but that's another story.

What has this got to do with exercise you might say? Well, in my enthusiasm to get shot of the guano on the fence, I inadvertently tripped over the coiled hose, causing me to fire a jet of cold water straight at next door's cat. Now cats, as you know, are not entirely partial to the wet stuff and can move very quickly when the mood takes them. Unfortunately, it was at the precise moment the soggy feline let out the strangest of noises and streaked across the driveway, that the inexperienced youth diverted his gaze to extract a leaflet to stuff through our letterbox.

I have to say he made a manful attempt to break his fall. However, the cat was having none of it and, taking offence to being stood on, left the boy with a nasty imprint of its nails as it scurried off to find solace in a nearby patch of catnip. To make matters worse, the lad also got a drenching as I tried to get the cat off him with what turned out to be a very inaccurate blast of water on my part.

Helping the still dazed youth to his feet, he murmured something about "cutting fat" or a least that's what I think he said as he handed me the leaflet, which was to lead to a most unfortunate set of events, of which more shortly. Just then Maude came out the house to, as she put it "find out what stupidity [I] had got up to this time.

Anyway, her attention on me soon waned as her gaze fixed on the youth, and in particular the trickle of blood oozing from the boy's forehead, which was dripping rhythmically from the tip of his nose and onto my driveway.

At this juncture she gave me one of her withering looks and, as her mothering instincts cut in, dragged the unwilling youth off to receive some care and attention, whether he wanted it or not. A few minutes later while I was busy blasting the last of the crap of my fence, I noticed the lad limping down the driveway at speed. He paused only the once to look over his shoulder at me.

I raised a hand to wish him good day. He raised a hand with the gesture more fitted to the football terraces. It was only when I went indoors that the full horror of what had taken place hit me.

Maude thrust the leaflet into my hand and announced we were to join an 'exercise for the over 50s' class. Now I don't know about you, Reg, but the wife and I have been around this block more than once before. Every Christmas Maude buys a fitness DVD by some so-called TV celebrity that you just know purposely piled on the pounds during the summer, just so the stupid woman could make a DVD showing you how she lost it again.

I have to say this doesn't fool me for a second. Nevertheless, come January 1st she makes me stand in front of the TV with her and flap my arms and legs about, like some demented parrot copying what its crazy owner is getting up to in the corner of the room.

To add insult to injury, when I collapse onto the sofa having had enough, Maude gives me a glance of derision and feigns exhilaration as she prances out of the room. I followed her once you know, only to find her collapsed and breathing heavily for oxygen in the kitchen.

And before you say it, I don't think the heavy breathing had anything to do with any form of carnal longings or suchlike. Realising she had been caught out; it was quite amusing to listen to her trying to talk normally, while gasping for air. Hang on, Reg, the phone's ringing, I'll email you back in a minute.

***

Hi Reg

I swear that if I get one more phone call from someone trying to order a Chinese takeaway I'll forward the call to the local branch of *Weight Watchers* out of spite. It doesn't matter how many times you tell people we're not the local takeaway, they'll insist we are and merrily attempt to hand over their credit card details. Of course, when it finally sinks in that they are not going to get their tea, they slam the phone down as if it's our fault.

Okay, let's talk exercise. Since the bird crap, cat, and grazed youth already cost me my lunch, I decided discretion being the better part of valour (and it being nearly teatime) I did as ordered by Maude and searched the inter-web thingy for exercise clothing. I have to say I felt this was an entirely unnecessary expense. However, Maude insisted that my current shorts would get me arrested for exposure if worn in public and that in any case, no one wore black plimsolls with grey ankle socks anymore.

I tell you, Reg, I gave Maude one of my fiercest looks to show my disapproval and if she had persisted, I would have waited until she was looking at me to make sure she knew I meant business. Let me ask you a question. How do you get on with this 'online' stuff? I only ask because in trying to do the right thing, I almost ended up being put out on the street by Maude.

I had meant to type into the search box (or whatever it is they call it), 'male kit for exercising'. However, after I put in the 'male kit' bit, the computer screen when bonkers, and changed in a flash to show a picture of a young women stretched out on a bed wearing less than an albino Mexican hairless dog. And I couldn't for the life of me work out what the bloke kneeling next to her was doing

Before I knew what was happening, the thing started playing a video. I have to say, the young people involved were doing the strangest exercises imaginable, with what appeared to be a pair of nutcrackers and a feather duster. What this has to do with exercise kit is quite beyond me. What's more, Maude walked in just as I was trying to decide what I should do next and accused me of being addicted to pornography.

As you know, Reg, for men of our age and disposition, the very last thing on our minds is pornography, and given the choice between that, and half an hour in our shed – the shed wins out every time. Besides which, if at any time I have the sensation of a bodily urge.

I find sucking on a bowl full of *Old Shag* in my favourite pipe for 10 minutes usually sorts things out. This state of affairs also seems to suit Maude, since she buys me copious quantities of the stuff, and is always asking if I need my pipes cleaning.

In any event the result was that Maude stormed out shouting something about my dinner being in the dahlias and that she would sort my new kit out herself.

Not to be outdone, I was determined to show her I could both master the inter-web and purchase fashionable exercise clothing. I've attached a picture to show you how I got on.

What do you think?

Needless to say, Maude was not particularly impressed and said that it looked as though I had fallen headfirst into a sock knitting machine. As you would expect, I brushed her cutting remark aside and put it down to her surprise (which she cunningly disguised) that I could do anything for myself – women just don't understand men do they, Reg. Anyway, I digress.

By last Thursday night the dreaded moment could be put off no longer as we walked through the doors of the (not so) leisure centre. There we stood in a huddle with eight other people who looked like clones of each other. The women all wearing a strange, not to say manic, look across their chops.

The men for the most part staring abjectly at the stained floor covering that masqueraded as a carpet (I'll swear those stains were from the tears of sobbing men of a certain age on their way in, and buckets of the sweat they deposited on their way out).

You know, Reg, the most depressing thing about these bloody centres is that they're filled with people who don't need to be there. You know the type; twenty-something, thin as a hungry chopstick and skin as orange as a carrot on steroids – that is until it rains.

At least I consoled myself in being a paragon of fitness when compared to some of the other poor men in our little cabal. Remember Alfie? You know the bloke who got done for incapacity benefit fraud for his bad back.

Well I guess he had a good run in getting away with it for 10 years when he didn't have a frozen spine at all, as proved by the video they took of him pole dancing in that dodgy club. As you may recall, the ironic thing is they made him take the first job that was offered to him, which, spookily, involved erecting lampposts.

Moreover, when he tried to show off to his workmates that he could shin up the things by the power of the thighs alone, he put his back out – but now no one believes him, especially his wife.

There he stood, groaning like a man being told to make the tea again by his wife, while she prodded him in the side and kept telling him to stand up straight. Queenie was also there but with a bloke I didn't recognise.

You might recall that she is now on her third husband, having worn the other two out with her unnatural urges for a woman of her age, size and looks. Perhaps Jason has gone the way of the other two and this bloke is his replacement. From the haunted expression on his face and her flushed cheeks, I don't think it will be long before number four makes his appearance.

It was at this point that I myself began to feel uncomfortable. Having been made by Maude to walk to the venue, my inner thighs were on fire from the chaffing of the very tight, high wasted shorts under my trousers – which she had assured me were all the rage.

So not only were my thighs on fire, meat and two veg in a state of turmoil and buttocks indignant at being cleaved apart, but the constant adjustments I had been making to alleviate the several sources of irritation had dislodged a heat patch I had carefully placed on my coccyx a couple of hours earlier.

Why the heat patch, I hear you say. In three words: Maude, ants and fire. The woman has a pathological dislike of the little blighters. Unfortunately, they have only disdain for her, and make a point of building nest after nest under her prized Chiminea on our patio. And so, as soon as she caught sight of the creatures, I was made to lift the Chiminea (which weighs a bloody ton), while she zeroed in on the entrance to the ant nest with my propane weed burner. Maude is hopeless with my propane weed burner.

As a consequence, she singed the toes of my left foot (as well as ruining the leather sandal they were nestled in) causing me to wince and drop the Chiminea – falling backwards as I did so onto the watering can containing boiling water, which Maude had strategically placed in order to boil the ants to death after she had burnt them to death. I have to say I don't know which was more painful, a metal waterspout in the coccyx, or boiling water up my arse. And before you say it, no, I am not a devotee of colonic irrigation – at any temperature.

To top it all, the result of Maude failing to take my cry of pain seriously, or pay attention to the descending patio heater, meant that the weed burner became trapped under the now cracked Chiminea, causing the handle of the thing to be wrenched from what were, until that moment, her immaculately manicured fingernails.

The result of Maude's cuticle disaster? Verdict: my fault. Sentence: another chicken-ding tea for me (what would us men do without microwaves, Reg?). So what happened to the heat patch? Well, it went walkabout down my trouser leg and emerged mischievously between my legs. Unfortunately, an over emotional woman to my right glanced the sudden movement, let out a shriek and accused me of appalling hygiene in displaying my incontinence pad to all and sundry.

I have to say, Reg, I do object at being pigeonholed by certain women who seem to think that any man in his seventh decade cannot exist without incontinence pads or little blue pills. Like you, I'm proud that I am in need of neither, since my bowels are in perfect working order – and separate bedrooms negate the need for the latter except on special occasions like the Queen's birthday. She has two a year, you know.

Reg, I'll need to get back to you, there seems to be a commotion in the kitchen. Speak soon.

**

…Back again, Reg. Drama over. It seems Maude's mother was choking on a handful of salted peanuts again. If I've told her once I've told her a hundred times that people without teeth have no right trying to eat such things. And the crazy woman's response? She says she needs the salt as it's good for her complexion, which, for a woman of ninety-eight leaves everything to the imagination, let me tell you.

I wouldn't mind if she'd limit herself to sucking one at a time. But she insists on packing her cheeks like a squirrel preparing for winter. The result? She sucks, she chokes, she spits – or to put it more precisely, she pebble-dashes anything and anyone who are in the line of fire. Most undignified if you ask me.

Now, where was I up to? Yes, incontinence. It goes without saying that Maude was not best pleased at being associated with a man who apparently flings such things around with gay abandon. So we were both thankful when the awkward silence and piercing glances were interrupted by two members of staff who didn't look old enough to cross the road on their own.

"We need to take some measurements before we take you through to the gym," announced one of the infants. "Now, who's first?"

Maude pushed me bodily forward and to be honest, I was glad to get away from the hysterical woman who refused to take her eyes off me. With defiance (and not inconsiderable pain), I bent down to pick up the offending heat patch, folded it neatly and placed it into my pocket with great ceremony.

The hysterical woman began to gag as she followed the square of material as it disappeared from sight. With that I pulled myself up to my full height, wincing only once or twice, and limped forward as I followed the child trainer into a small room, the entrance door of which had 'constipation room' written on it. I suspect this had not been the original spelling used to denote the room's purpose.

"The first thing we need to do is to check your body mass index," said she.

I have to say, Reg, I was a little taken back and completely misunderstood what the young woman was referring to. I'm afraid things went from bad to worse when I said the volume and weight of my private parts were really none of her concern.

It didn't help matters when at precisely that moment she popped a boiled sweet into her mouth. I much admired her ability to narrow her eyes and curl her upper lip as she let out a throaty cough. In the process, she expelled the confectionery with such velocity that it left a visible mark as it pinged off a rather grubby little mirror, knocked out one of three light bulbs and miraculously found its way into an otherwise empty wastepaper basket.

Do you think that's what women mean by multitasking?

Misunderstanding overcome and once she had recovered her composure, the woman instructed me to stand on some scales (which, if I may say so, told lies), then gestured me to stand against the wall while she measured my height. She scribbled the results on a badly photocopied form and with the aid of a calculator (why can't young people do mental arithmetic anymore?), then announced that my 'B M I' was over 30 which is apparently, a very bad thing.

I disputed both my recorded weight and in particular, my height, and told her that I was both lighter and longer in the morning, but that I got very stiff first thing.

For some bizarre reason she berated me for using inappropriate language and said that if I didn't desist immediately, she would bring the assessment to a conclusion and call the police. Just at that moment Maude entered the room (without first knocking I should add) to announce that the rest of the group had been assessed and were waiting for me. Seeing the awkwardness of the situation, she immediately assumed I had insulted the young woman and accepted her side of events.

Tutting while simultaneously fixing her eyes on the broken light bulb, at which she squinted curiously for a few seconds; there followed an exchange of knowing glances between the two women, then they half turned their faces (slowly followed by their eyes) in my direction and gave a sort of 'harrumph' sound in unison. Women are the most curious things are they not, Reg?

As Maude began to usher me out of the room with a less than gentle prod to the small of my back, the young woman suggested I might like to purchase a supply of detox pills. I immediately knew that this was my chance to reclaim the upper hand.

"I have absolutely no need for such medication and do not take drugs of any sort, young lady," I announced.

With that I left the room without giving the woman a second glance. Though I did get a further prod from Maude in exactly the same spot that her earlier poke had landed (I am certain this is a skill all women are born with).

***

Returning from the changing room with the glories of my new gym kit exposed for all to wonder at, I was pulled up with a start as I glimpsed the most extraordinary sight. While I had had grave doubts concerning Maude's fashion sense (not least her ability to determine what size shorts I wore), I felt positively 'on trend' when compared to the odd assortment of oversized tops and outsized tracksuit bottoms my compatriot men were wearing.

And as for the women – I leave it to your imagination, Reg. Suffice to say that skin tight lycra and an overabundance of wobbly bits do no favours, for either the fabric or its contents.

Anyway, after Maude had made yet another hurtful remark about my headband making me remove it on pain of cooking my own supper, I stuffed it down the front of my now even tighter shorts.

Inexplicably, Maude shot me one of her death stares – yet when I retrieved the still dry accessory and tried to hand it to her for safe storage, she swatted my hand away with the deftest flick of her extended fingers. Fortunately, I was quickly able to regain ownership of the thing before the old gentleman whose bald head it had landed on realised what had happened.

I have to say that I thought it was very clever of the group organiser to distract attention from Maude's folly while I retrieved my headband, by announcing that we should all follow her for a tour around the exercise equipment.

A piece of advice, Reg. Do not enter such a place if you wish to minimise any re-occurrence of those haemorrhoids that I know are often your companion. Have you any idea the mauling that your not-so-little friends would suffer as the cheeks of your backside rhythmically clenched and cleaved at the behest of sundry exercise bikes and rowing machines? Well, Reg, from the look on the faces of the fools that I saw, it really is something best avoided.

It was taking pity on one such lady who had left the first flushes of youth in the lost property department of the Victoria and Albert Museum, which got me into trouble. In my defence, she looked bored to tears limping with both feet on a treadmill, while staring intently at the digital readout which she was also using to keep herself upright.

As it turned out she was, in fact, trying to free a rather delicate (though clearly strong) neck chain that had become entangled with the control panel of the infernal machine. Seeing the danger of the situation, I immediately tried to untangle the chain. I did think it rather odd that the more robustly I attempted to free her, the more intently she stared at me, and more laboured her breathing became.

As I look back on the situation I can see my error in focusing so intently on resolving matters meant I inadvertently rested my palm on the speed button – and the luckless woman had to trot ever faster to stay in the same place.

So, you can see that in my moment of triumph, the very act of freeing the unfortunate woman's head, led to failure. She shot back at some speed, tripped backwards as her feet met with the stationary floor and was launched headfirst (with a sort of half-pike turn) into the crotch of a very surprised young man undertaking a most peculiar floor exercise, which involved being in a seated position with both arms behind him and legs akimbo.

Aside from the hush that descended on the gymnasium, it's hard to say who of the two was more surprised, or indeed, in more pain. Nevertheless, the young man was most gracious in helping the elderly lady to her feet – which to be fair, took some time. I was particularly impressed that he readjusted her wig without anybody but me noticing.

The feat was all the more impressive given his own discomfiture, which was only evident by the tears rolling gently down his cheeks and slightly ruddy complexion (which I suspect had nothing to do with any notion of sexual excitement).

In any event, I averted my eyes since I thought this was a gentlemanly thing to do, and instead busied myself engaging a nearby gym instructor in the finer points of effort expended in return for calories discarded. Although a little bemused by the events taking place behind me, he was nevertheless able to respond to my questions, even if he was staring blankly into space just clear of my right ear. Having asked him how long I would have to pedal like Billy O on one of their exercise bikes to rid myself of 250 calories, he responded in a rather robotic voice…

"40 minutes."

His voice tailed off as he regained his focus and rather ungraciously looked me up and down, before adding, "Or in your case, an hour."

It seemed to me, Reg, that the man's response was absurd. I said that if he had been in the return on investment business he'd have gone bankrupt a long time ago. It was at this point I noticed the ever-present Maude staring intently at me. However, undeterred I told him that I would rather eat one meat and potato pie less and save what was left of my knee joints than take those odds.

Before the man could defend his position, Maude sidled up to me and (rather spitefully, I thought), found her favourite landing point in the middle of my back again with the tip of her finger.

Needless to say, I was not prepared to be silenced, and informed the trainer that in any case, and since I was somewhat of an expert on exercise equipment, the centre needed to pay more attention to health and safety matters.

By way of example I drew the man's attention to the elderly gentleman who had earlier, albeit for a fleeting moment, worn my headband and who, given his bulging eyeballs and tepid complexion, was now clearly struggling on a cross trainer.

You should know, Reg, that it was not my intention to surprise the old bloke who was by now panting more heavily than your Labrador lying in front of the gas fire on a summer's day.

Indeed, my only thought, as I lightly rested a hand on his white knuckles, was to offer him reassurance. Alas my kind act seemed to break his concentration as he jumped in surprise, let go of the weightlifting bar and sprang upwards and forwards as the leg resistors pushed his feet behind him.

Luckily both the trainer and I reacted instantaneously and with great athleticism by grabbing an arm each, thereby ending the man's short flight and resting him back into the seat of the cross trainer, where he remained very quietly for quite some time.

All's well that ends well I say, Reg.

However, if that wasn't enough excitement for one night, later on the situation went from the sublime to the ridiculous. As the elderly man from the cross trainer gathered his wits, picked up his walking stick and stumbled rather awkwardly towards the bar, an extremely portly bloke bounded into the gymnasium with all the fleetness of foot of a bull elephant on heat.

"Over 50s fitness fans, please gather round."

His announcement was met with complete bemusement until one of the trainers made it clear, with an outstretched and pointing finger, who he was addressing his comments to. So, the ten of those (less the old bloke hiding in the bar) gathered around the fat one like a group of school kids waiting to be told by the teacher who was to be in detention that day.

"I want to tell you how very pleased I am that so many of you have responded to my fantastic keep fit initiative. As we get older it is something we all have to pay great attention to, as is the importance we need to place on keeping our weight under control."

It was at this point, Reg, that I'd had enough. While the trainers struggled to repress their sniggers, the rest of the group looked at the floor and Maude glared at me in that 'don't you dare speak' sort of way.

Undeterred, I stopped the fat one in full flow by asking him why he felt qualified to lecturer us in the finer points of fitness and diet. I think it worth quoting his response verbatim, since you are the one who is always banging on about the worthiness of politicians.

"I, sir, am the cabinet member of your County Council with specific responsibility for lifelong fitness through partnership and multi-agency working with key stakeholders, to deliver key outcomes and outputs via public sector engagement with our customers; remembering always that our primary driver is equality of access, the celebration of diversity and to encourage underrepresented groups and individuals to participate in cross community initiatives thereby enhancing cohesion and sustainability."

Believe it or not he finished without taking a breath by adding…

"And anyway, we got some cash from Europe which has to be spent by March or we lose it."

All now became clear, Reg, as did the little 'goody bag' we were given earlier containing a crappy blue flag and a 'your guide to the European Community: benefits of membership' glossy book.

I had to bite my tongue in not asking him to repeat himself – but this time in plain English, since I'd long come to the conclusion that politicians spent their life jibbajabbing to each other in lala land, while obsessing over their expenses claim forms, rather than actually doing anything for real people.

Suffice to say, I thanked him for breaking the world record for the number of words spoken without taking a breath and suggested that given his enthusiasm for keep fit activities, he should demonstrate his commitment by taking a turn on the rowing machine that cowered beside him.

Fair play to the pompous bugger, he lowered his massive backside onto the seat which I swear made an attempt to escape from certain suffocation, wedged his ample shoes into the foot straps and grabbed the oars with enough force to row the Atlantic in one stroke. It seemed to me that in an attempt to show us he was well practiced in using the machine that he overreached himself. The audible gasp from all assembled which followed shortly after was in response to him letting go of the oars on the backstroke, so to speak.

Unfortunately for him, his feet remained wedged in their restraints, meaning that his ample torso shot back, rendering him in a state of unconsciousness as his head took a glancing blow from the first aid cabinet, which had been thoughtfully placed immediately behind the machine.

To add to his embarrassment, as he came round, he murmured his thanks for being slapped by a lady called pussykins and asked that she hit him harder, but would she please untie his feet as it was cutting off the blood supply.

Luckily, the paramedics were already on hand attending the woman on the exercise bike and the old man who was still refusing to come out of the bar. Needless to say, the fat councillor's (reminds me of a children's book about trains, Reg,) attempt to kiss the female paramedic didn't go down too well, and I am sure in the eyes of some, her pouring such a large quantity of disinfectant into his not insignificant wound with such gusto was entirely justifiable.

The question it raised for me, however, was whether he actually enjoyed the additional pain he was now experiencing. Nevertheless, it seemed to do the trick as far as his roving hands were concerned.

...Will need to get back to you, Reg, I think a Courier has just delivered my new vacuum pump for the air conditioning unit.

***

I'm back, Reg. Sorry it took so long but I've just had the most extraordinary experience and Maude has gone into a steep decline. You know when I said to you earlier that I wasn't very good with this inter-web stuff. Well it turns out that the vacuum pump I *thought* I'd ordered turned out to be a very different sort of pump altogether.

Unfortunately, Maude took the box from the Courier and went into the kitchen because she thought it was a new rolling pin that *she* had ordered. As usual, she didn't bother to check the name on the package before opening it (a source of great contention, Reg), and got more than she bargained for when she emptied the contents onto the kitchen table. It was at this point I heard her scream.

"And your reason for buying this is…"

In addition, the mother-in-law let out a gummy shriek.

Believe you me, Reg, I didn't get fully through the kitchen door before Maude threw the packaging at me and held up a glass contraption with a rubber tube sticking out of one end, to which a hand pump was attached.

"Think very carefully how you say what you are about to say to me," said Maude.

"It's for the air conditioning unit?" I replied before actually looking at what she was on about.

"And where exactly do you fit a penis enlargement pump in the air conditioning system?" she said sarcastically.

At this point Maude's mother gave another little gummy shriek, took a lingering look at the glass tube, then ran out of the kitchen in a hobbley sort of way with more than a glint in her one remaining good eye. I tell you, Reg, it took me some while to convince Maude that I pressed the wrong 'buy' button on the computer, and that she knew quite well that I had absolutely no need of a glass tube, replete or not with a pump for my little chap to become a big chap.

All I can say is thank the Lord for separate bedrooms and the Queen only having two birthdays a year. Anyway, enough of all that and I was sure Maude would find her mother before she managed to get her arthritic hands on any unsuspecting male now that her blood was up (they tend to lock in position every now and again you know, so I had to hope she didn't manage to grab any poor bloke's manhood).

As far as the battle clearing station that was the leisure centre was concerned, I'm pleased to say that one of the trainers took the initiative and suggested that as a group we retired to the bar while they cleared things up.

With that, and the nine of us needing no further encouragement, we made ourselves comfortable with alcohol and a party bag of pork scratchings. The moment was interrupted only by the old bloke, who you may remember had been hiding in the bar, making a surprisingly swift exit as he saw us approach.

After a few minutes I glimpsed half a dozen youngsters at the other end of the room doing what I assume were warm up exercises before they joined their class.

I say warm up exercises in the loosest possible sense, since the positions some of their number were able to achieve had more in common with a contortionist having lost all sense of reality. Intrigued, I engaged them in discussion asking them how long they had been doing gymnastics and the like. I have to say that in complete contradiction of the stereotype some (of course not you and I) apply to young people; they were the epitome of good manners and courtesy.

After asking me the usual questions one gets from anyone under 10 years of age, you know the type...

What did you do in the war?

What was it like before cars were invented?

How did you talk to each other before *iPhones* were invented?

...I began to lose the plot as they started talking in a sort of code. When I asked one of them if he enjoyed coming to the centre, the lad said he thought it was 'nang' which believe it or not means 'excellent', and that it was a good way of avoiding a 'bacon bandage' which apparently describes an overabundance of flesh around the midriff.

In a vain attempt to keep the conversation going in such a way as not to let slip that I didn't have the foggiest what they were talking about, I said that their fitness training regime at least kept them off the streets.

"Yeah, it's 404 to hang around and anyway the helicopters are always bugging you," replied one of the girls.

"I agree, it's swag," said another.

You'll be interested to know, Reg, that 404 is derived from a computer failure and 'helicopters' are parents who demand to know where their children are at all times. As for 'swag', well, it's beyond me.

Feeling a little light headed and the need for beer, I brought the conversation to an end by throwing in a general, "good, so you'd rather be here then?"

"It's epic – you know, shining," said the smallest amongst them as he picked up a mobile phone that was nearly as big as the lad himself. As if on cue, it began to ring out to the theme tune to *Only Fools and Horses*, which I thought quite quaint, since even the repeats of this program started before the youngster was born.

Ah well, who says they don't teach history at school anymore.

I retreated to the bar. But before I could get my order in, one of the trainers appeared and suggested that we all might like to join her back on the training floor – which didn't appeal to me, or my companions judging by the look on their faces as they tried to un-stick their teeth from the pork scratchings.

Nevertheless, closely escorted by Maude I, along with the rest of our hapless band, did as instructed. It's worth noting that the staff had made a very nice job of removing any trace of the bodily fluids which had been spilled by the casualties such a short time earlier.

Ordering us into a line, the trainer announced that we were to be put through a routine of 'gentle' arm and leg exercises – wait for it, Reg, – to music! So there the trainer stood, stop watch in hand like a human timer waiting for the turkey to cook, while one of her compatriots stood immediately in front of us bidding we follow her every move when the music started.

A question, Reg. What sort of music would you have in mind to encourage a bunch of people to exercise who would never see sixty again? *Moon River?* A touch of *Russ Conway?* Or perhaps a dash of *Slade's greatest hits?* Not a bit of it. Instead the trainer launched into a manic routine to the accompaniment of *A Bat Out Of Hell* by *Meatloaf.*

As the youngsters I had spoken to earlier might have said: 404.

What followed can only be described as a car crash. Picture the scene if you will. The trainer almost taking off trying to keep up with the blasted music that was so loud it could have been designed to push up the sales of Tinnitus medication.

And us lot, tripping over each other trying to coordinate hands and feet that hadn't got a clue who *Meatloaf* was. I don't know who was more relieved when the music finished, trainer, or the first aiders who had been sat pensively in one corner after their earlier interventions.

At any rate, the now puce looking trainer who had been leading the exercise then suggested in a very breathy voice that we should next do a 'warm down' exercise. By this time, I think we'd all had enough and were in no mood for warming of any sort.

Nevertheless, the trainer insisted we should follow her example which would, she said, help to bring our breathing back under control. It seemed to me that the only thing that could do this was an oxygen mask. However, given no such equipment was readily to hand we gave her the benefit of the doubt.

Seeing that she had achieved compliance (which in reality had more to do with our inability to move a muscle), she told us to watch her complete the exercise before attempting it ourselves. With that, she pulled herself up to her full extent, lifted her arms and stretched these behind her head, ending up in a sort of arch like a position with her head tilted back and eyes staring at the ceiling.

I suppose we should have known better, but thinking we would be allowed to go home after this last few minutes of unpleasantness, the group did as they were told and tried to replicate the ridiculous posture the trainer had ended up in.

It didn't take long for two of our number to topple backwards like a colony of penguins trying to look up at a passing aeroplane and ending up flat on their backs for their trouble.

I suspect the trainer at this point knew she had gone too far and suggested that we all sit on the floor (which we declined for reasons of dignity and brittle bones) to rest, while the now very jittery first aiders reluctantly came out of their corner and comforted our fully reclined colleagues.

The two of them were by now moaning in unison, which, to my surprise, was quite tuneful and not at all unpleasant on the ear. In any event within a few minutes, relative health and fresh supplies to the first aid cabinet were restored, which seemed to be the signal to our trainer that she should once again rally us around.

All in all this was successful, save for the two penguins who still seemed a little dazed as they hung onto one another for dear life; their gaze firmly fixed on the floor.

For some madcap reason the trainer thought it would be a good idea that we should do one last circuit of the gymnastics equipment to, as she put it, "finish off the evening with a flourish."

I am pleased to say that the ladies, of whom Maude was in the forefront, refused saying that it was out of the question, on account that *Dallas* was on the telly within the hour. I have to say, Reg, I've never been a fan of the series since *Bobby* was reborn in the shower – do script writer's think we're stupid? As far as I was concerned, that evening's episode of dark doings at *Southfork* was just at this moment THE most important thing in my life if it saved me from further physical exertion – which would inevitably lead to an argument with my varicose veins, not to mention inflaming the still tender toes of my left foot from Maude's earlier crap aim with the weed burner.

***

Realising that the game was up, the trainer capitulated on the further exercise idea and asked us to meet in the bar when, as she put it, we had 'freshened up'. Given the sickly aroma of sweat that hangs in the air in these places, I decided it wasn't worth the trouble and headed for the bar, and before Maude could yank me towards the men's changing room.

Eventually the rest turned up and Maude sat some distance away from me. In walked the trainer with a handheld credit card terminal and some threatening looking forms tucked under one armpit, which still bore a damp patch from her attempt to keep up with *Meatloaf.*

Now the sales pitch came…

"We very much hope you enjoyed your time with us this evening," said the young woman. "And I hope that you have all caught the exercise bug. Now with that in mind we have a very special offer that I'd like to tell you about, but before I do, I would just like to show you pictures of some of our other mature members, so you can see what the centre can do for you."

When I asked what had happened to Europe in that I thought we were being offered a free course, she replied that the scheme only applied to those under 16, since 'they' had given up trying to bribe old people about the merits of the European Community.

While I agree with her sentiment, Reg, I did ask her to explain the purpose of the goody bags and what the hell the fat controller and been talking about. She said that they had more goody bags than they knew what to do with, so gave them to anyone who passed the reception desk.

As for the counsellor, she said that she, too, had been a little confused and thought he had wanted to talk to us about the new care home shortly to open in the village.

Had it not been for the group being more interested in sinking as much alcohol as possible before *Dallas* started, I suspect there would have been more of a reaction to what the young woman was saying. In any event, she charged on regardless by passing around the photographs. These took the form of a series of 'before and after' images purporting to show the benefits of exercise for the likes of you and me.

I have to say, Reg, that the 'after' photographs of the men made their faces look like a bag of spanners and their ruddy complexion redolent of too much gin. As for the women, suffice to say, their skin looked like it needed a good ironing, and most of them had those strange staring eyes, which if your better half is anything like Maude, means only one thing…

'Get back into your shed and out of my way before I put another laxative in your tea.'

As you would expect, I asked if there were any discounts for pensioners. She replied that in normal circumstances it was not possible to offer a discount, since the average attendance for this age group was nine months and then they never saw them again.

It seems it cost the centre good money trying to discover which care home they had been moved into. Before I or anyone else could object to the slanderous stereotype, she raced on to say that by special permission (she didn't say whom), she had been authorised to offer two years membership for the price of one.

I challenged her by asking what was the point of offering us a two-year membership if we were all to be gaga within nine months?

Clearly thinking on her feet and doing a vault fast on her earlier assertion, she said in all seriousness and without batting an eyelid...

"Of course, you will still be able to visit the centre as long as you have a Carer with you; supply of incontinence pads and a change of clothing."

Just then I noticed that one of the other men was weeping into a paper tissue.

"Now look what you've done," I said to the trainer, at which point the old bloke spoke up in a garbled sort of voice...

"I don't give a toss about the keep fit thing, I've just bitten my tongue with my stupid new dentures – they've got a bloody life of their own."

I should add, Reg, that he could only say this by taking his teeth out and handing them to his clearly annoyed wife, as he dabbed a paper tissue that had seen better days onto his tongue to mop up the blood.

Embarrassed by having to hold her husband's bloodstained teeth, one set in each hand, it seemed to me she was intent on revenge. I noticed that as she handed them back to him (point-blank refusing to handle the blooded tissue) she swapped them around meaning his top denture was now his bottom set, and vice versa.

You wouldn't believe the colour he turned as he forced his now ill-fitting dentures onto his gums. I thought he was going to pass out as he gagged on a mixture of blood from the reopened wound on his tongue, saliva and his upper teeth, which were clearly intent on regaining their rightful position.

The heady mix of being insulted by the trainer and the ghastly image of the gagging man fighting with his teeth, led to half the group scarpering before the trainer could get to them.

When I told the young lady that I wished to think further about membership, Maude raised her eyes to the ceiling (unfortunately she did not succumb to the falling backwards thing), while two other men signed up under duress from their wives and with clearly shaking hands – which I suspect had nothing to do with any medical or alcohol related illness.

***

Just to round this little escapade off, I should say that Maude tends to be a little hyper first thing in the morning and talks incessantly over the breakfast table – which drives me to distraction. However, the next day she seemed in an unduly reflective mood. Initially I thought this may have been due to her mother almost having sexually assaulted a young man who happened to be passing the drive the previous evening (remember I told you about the glass tube?).

I then thought it may also have been due to her pondering where her mother had managed to find a fresh supply of salted peanuts – which she quickly removed from the woman and replaced them with a bowl of fruit salad (shorn of their skins of course). It was then that I realised where Maude acquired her dreaded 'death stare' that usually meant I needed to get out of the house.

…It was of course from her mother (who refused to eat the fruit salad and tossed it over Maude's favourite dry flower arrangement). It seems, Reg, the old adage that we grow into our parents has some semblance of truth, God help us (since you know what my father turned into – what with the sheep and all). As it turned out, Maude was playing her old game of double bluff.

Her quiet demeanour had nothing to do with her mother, peanuts or pump enhanced glass tube, and everything to do with tricking me into signing up for those stupid exercise classes. I'm proud to say that I stood my ground, saying that I was still very stiff from the exertions of the previous evening (though I suspect this had more to do with the Chiminea business).

I added that I would rather do the painting and decorating (which as you know I've trained Maude not to trust me to do), than give money away to be ritually humiliated; lose the weight I've spent years putting on in case of sudden famine conditions, or tone muscles I've spent years getting rid of.

I also had in mind, Reg, that the development of certain muscle tone has a direct link to the production of testosterone and all that sex urge stuff that goes with it. This, of course, would directly interfere with the time I could otherwise put to good use in the shed. What was Maude's response you may ask? Curiously little – at least that's what I thought at the time. She muttered something about finding other ways to get me fit.

Thinking she was talking about the bedroom department, I undertook to hide my stock of little blue pills – which should not be interpreted as any disloyalty toward the Monarchy, or indeed, disrespect to either of Her Majesty's Birthdays.

A few days later I noticed a familiar looking leaflet distributor walking somewhat gingerly up the drive, almost as if he was looking for something.

By way of being friendly I waved to him from the window, which seemed to motivate the young man to quicken his pace to our letterbox, stuff something through it and run back down the drive without acknowledging me at all.

Young people really are difficult to fathom are they not, Reg?

Unbeknown to me, Maude had seen the lad and insisted that the youth was the same chap who had suffered the unfortunate run in with next door's cat and who had caught a good soaking from my pressure washer.

Quite unfairly I think, she said that I had probably scarred him for life and put him in fear of going anywhere near water in the future. This was something I was not having, Reg, and said that an aversion to water was the perfectly natural state of affairs for all teenage boys, who make up for their lack of hygiene by spraying deodorant over the clothes they are wearing, rather than risking any contact with the skin.

At that point, Maude's mother came into the room, handed her the leaflet and spat a salt-less peanut at me. Maude was a little too excited for my liking and I now realised the evil plan she had been hatching over the breakfast table as she first read, then held aloft, the leaflet, declaring…

"It's either Zumba classes or we get the bikes out again."

I'll finish, Reg, by attaching a photograph of the cycle helmet Maude has made me wear.

END

3 The Crabby Old Git on Weddings

Dear Reg,

Thanks for your email and it was a shame you weren't able to get to the wedding. You didn't miss much, apart from Maude getting drunk, her mother molesting the vicar and my niggling doubt as to whether the Bride and Groom got married in a legal sense at all. Come to think of it, you were probably safer stuck at home in your neck brace. Speaking of which, how is your whiplash?

I won't trot out the usual depraved jokes about leather straps, rubber masks and nail-lined underpants, which I know you're not into – despite scurrilous rumours in the village to the contrary (which I have to say, you are not helping yourself by clearing Gerard's DIY emporium of brass tacks and 'weld your fingers together' superfast glue).

You really should tell Podgy Gerard about your furniture upholstery hobby, rather than teasing him about some imaginary fetish that as a married man you probably have no need of – unless there's something you want to tell me?

Podgy, on the other hand, being the frustrated bachelor on account of his mother's terror that one of her kind (if it's possible two such beings should exist) might come between her and golden balls, has every incentive to fantasise whenever the opportunity arises.

So, if I were you, I'd stick to buying clothes pegs and garden twine off him now that the good weather has arrived. On reflection, why not stay clear of him altogether, since it will only feed his passions as he conjures up a mental image of you being tied to a bed post having your men's bits clamped to some electrical implement or other.

Anyway, only another couple of weeks before your neck brace comes off and by then the police should have stopped laughing at your Judith's explanation as to why she hit that bus when she reversed out of your drive. Is she really going to stick to her story that it couldn't possibly have been her fault on account that the number 23 was 10 minutes early? I can see the delicate position this put you in. If you agree with her, it will only encourage Judith to keep driving, which I know is a terrifying prospect.

On the other hand, if you try saying you didn't see anything on account of having your head in your hands and anyway, you were busy grinding a hole in the mat pressing the non-existent brake, you risk microwaving your own chicken-ding meals for the next month.

What the hell, you like microwaved chicken don't you?

Of course, there's an upside. You have the insurance claim to look forward to, even if it does involves suing your own wife. Think about it, Reg. What greater pleasure could there be for a bloke to get money out of his wife for a change. What's more, for once you'll be *paid* for getting it in the neck, if you see what I mean.

...And the wedding? While, as you know, I am something of an expert when it comes to this sort of thing, the prospect of actually having to go to one makes my varicose veins go into spasm at the thought of standing for hours; talking to relatives

I can't stand (and would rather chew used cat litter than converse with); buying rounds of drinks for people I've never met in my life and tell porky pies about how lovely it is to see everybody again.

...And anyway, who the hell gets married in February? I bet it was Trevor's idea since no doubt it would have been cheaper than a summer do, and the nutter would have thought snowdrifts in every photograph would in some way look romantic. If I'm being honest, it was something of a surprise to receive the invitation in the first place. Then again, Cousin Trevor couldn't resist the calculated snub of addressing the invite to 'Maude + one'.

You know that we haven't got on since he organised my stag do and arranged that 'surprise' police stripogram. You'll recall that what he didn't tell me was the uniform I started to undo was still attached to a real police officer. When I got arrested for assault and carrying out an indecent act on a WPC, he scarpered with the 'real' stripogram to play 'stroke my truncheon' around the back of that Chinese takaway.

At least there was justice in him taking rather more away than he bargained for. How he kept his visits to that clinic from the clueless Cleo is beyond me – then again, he always was a slippery sod. You may also remember *your* shoddy excuse for not helping me out since you were asleep on top of a bus shelter, on account that you were waiting for a double-decker?

Suffice to say in spite me asking the WPC if she would like me to blow into her whistle, after an hour or so in the cells they took pity on me. More likely they were petrified by the look Maude gave the desk sergeant (you see even at that early stage in our relationship, Maude had perfected that bloody 'death stare') and let me go.

And here I have to agree with your philosophy in life that revenge is best served cold, or at least sober. It still gives me the greatest satisfaction that I managed to track down that stripogram and send her to Trevor's place, which you may remember, he had only just moved into with Mrs Clueless.

That stripogram played a blinder as the vacuum cleaner demonstrator Trevor thought I'd sent, because I told him Maude and I would buy any model they wanted as a wedding present. I wish I could have been a fly on the wall as she stripped while demonstrating its accessory kit.

Personally, I'm surprised Cleo ever got over it enough to get pregnant after what I told the stripogram to do with the upholstery brush. Then again, perhaps it gave them some ideas since Trevor never did have much gumption. And so, as you know, nine months later Jane was born.

At any rate the girl survived, has apparently prospered and has been daft enough to hitch herself to an environmental activist from Notting Hill. If nothing else I'm sure she'll enjoy her honeymoon hanging off a zip wire in wellington boots and bobble hat during their stay at the M93 protest camp.

Anyway, having accepted Trevor's invitation, Maude made me go shopping with her to buy an electric blanket for the happy couple. Let me ask you a question, Reg.

How many types of electric blanket do you think it's possible to buy? Well, after two hours being dragged from one shop to another I stopped counting at 24. More than that, I now feel able to write a magazine column on the merits and dangers of plugging the marital bed into the National Grid.

As Maude interrogated one disinterested young shop assistant after another as to why she should buy this blanket rather than that blanket, I couldn't help wondering why a newly married couple would need an electrical appliance of any sort in bed. Maude and I have managed quite well enough over the last 45 years without the need for a three-pin socket attached to the eiderdown, batteries or any other type of appliance to get a good night's sleep (earplugs excepted of course).

Then again, perhaps today's young women are more demanding than was the case when we were lads – I have certainly heard rumours to this effect and there is no doubt that in this respect Maude has been a late developer (thank heavens).

What am I talking about? I'm glad you asked. Well, as I trooped behind Maude and entered the umpteenth bed store, I noticed a young lady a few feet behind me. Naturally, I held the door open for her only to be accused of being a sexist pig and that she was quite capable of opening the thing herself.

Priding myself at being able to take a hint, I let go of the door since the woman clearly wanted to show me that she knew how to use a door handle. Unfortunately, it slammed shut rather more quickly than I or, I suspect, the young woman, expected. The blood and snot didn't half leave a mess on the door as it smacked her in the nose. I have to say that if you ignored her bodily fluids running down the glass, looking at her face you would have been hard pressed to notice trauma of any sort.

Now you might say that may have been on account of her inherited looks, about which she could do little. I suspect it was actually more to do with the layers of makeup and spray-on suntan, which had done a magnificent job in holding the bits of her nose together.

To cap it all she shouted in a most unladylike way that I was an inconsiderate sod and a banker – or a least that's what it sounded like, though why she thought I worked in the financial sector is quite beyond me since I wasn't wearing a Bowler hat or anything.

It did strike me as a sign of the times that as she wobbled a couple of loose teeth with one hand, the thumb on the other hand was moving at the speed of light across the keypad of her iPhone thingy.

I suspect she was nattering, or twattering (or whatever they call it) to the universe that she had been assaulted by one of those nasty bankers – well they do get the blame for everything these days don't they. So there you have it. You open the door for a woman and you are being sexist. You close the door so the woman can open it herself and you are a banker. What on earth is a man to do, I ask?

For once I was grateful that Maude took charge and dragged me away from what was a very tense situation. Nevertheless, I did think she went too far when she said to the young girl (with rather too much conviction for my liking), that I couldn't help myself on account of my excitement of being out of the care home, and that I would be back under sedation before the day was out.

Maude stared straight at me as she spoke, with those piercing eyes that could reduce the Medusa to tears, daring me to contradict her. It won't surprise you to learn, Reg, that I decided to rise above the game being played out amongst the two women. Instead, I instigated a tactical withdrawal by feigning interest amongst a nearby display of boxed candles (though curiously the instructions for use pointed out that batteries were not included).

I therefore undertook by way of retribution to increase the dose of self-administered bromide I slipped into any hot drink Maude made for me for a month. At least one of us would get a good kip for a change.

Anyway, once the kerfuffle died down, Maude pulled me away from the candles that needed batteries (but curiously looked over her shoulder at the display several times as we left the shop) and, you guessed it, we ended up at the first shop we'd gone in two hours previously. And it was there that the ordeal I had been nervously waiting for took place.

"Which one of these two do you prefer," said Maude, holding up a pink box and a blue box.

I know that we have discussed the matter many times and come to the conclusion that the counter-intuitive response is usually the safer one. In this case my first reaction being 'the blue one', I said 'the pink one'. And do you know, Reg, for once it worked! I managed to get away with...

"You're only saying that because you want to get home so you can disappear into your shed."

Well, Reg, given the morning I'd had, I was more than happy to settle for a death stare and being dismissed with an imperious wave of Maude's right hand as she swatted me out of the way, demanded my credit card and launched herself on yet another uninterested young shop assistant.

...I'll get back in a minute, Reg. It sounds like the mother-in-law has cornered the electric meter reading man under the stairs again.

**

...Well, that was a close call. I've told Maude time and time again to make sure her mother is locked in her granny flat when the meter man's due. I wouldn't mind, but I've only just persuaded the company to sanction meter readings again after that nasty incident when the old girl offered to hold the meter man's torch.

I can still see the look on his face as she made a grab for his meat and two veg. while the silly sod innocently replied that he could manage quite well with his torch. A saving grace was that, as you know, mother-in-law doesn't have any teeth, so *had* she managed to get to grips (so to speak) with the terrified meter reader's manhood, she wouldn't have left any physical marks.

On this occasion she tried her favoured 'rear entry' trick. No sooner had the new bloke bent down to read the meter and she was between his legs grabbing a good handful.

And you will remember from your own unfortunate encounters with her, that once her hands are clasped, they are more difficult to prise apart than a Yorkshire Clam. Now under our stairs is not a big place, and within a nanosecond of his natural reaction to having his nuts felt, he bolted forward cracking his head on a stair riser.

Anyway, once I'd managed to prise the toothless assassin off her prey and told Maude to bribe her with softened chocolate macaroons to get her out of the room, the young man was none the worse for wear. He just looked a bit confused as to why he was having to pick himself up off the floor.

As he crawled back out from under the stairs, I told him he'd tripped over Maude's stash of tinned tuna which she keeps in case of famine, civil unrest or coalition government. It's worth noting, Reg, that I detest tuna and can't digest the stuff. Poor bloke, I'm not sure he believed me for a second, but in the absence of having his own explanation, he hobbled out of the house massaging the bump on his head with one hand, while cupping his nuts with the other.

I thought the least I could do was to carry his meter reading gizmo back to the car. Curiously, 20 minutes later, I noticed that he was still staring blankly into space as he clasped the steering wheel with both hands as if his life depended on it. Well, back to the wedding. Maude had decided we were going and said that she also wanted to take her mother. As you can imagine,

I gave her that 'you must be joking after last time' sort of look, but she was adamant. And I know which wars to fight – this was not one of them.

Nevertheless, there were a couple of 'lines in the sand' which I made plain had to be met if 'mother' was to come with us. Number 1 was the type of accommodation that we would stay in. Surprisingly, Maude agreed quite readily that the rooms between the mother-in-law and us should have adjoining doors, so we could keep an eye on what she was up to.

Perhaps it was because she had no wish for a rerun of the near catastrophe her mother caused last time we were away. You may remember the rather unfortunate incident when the old woman ordered room service and was stark naked by the time the waiter arrived with her sausage and mash.

I didn't believe her for a minute when she said she had been doing her yoga exercises; for one thing she can't lift either leg off the floor without falling flat on her back – which is not a pretty sight when her version of a leotard is a pair of oversize bloomers and one of my old string vests.

In the event, it was lucky I happened to be passing her room when I heard the most bloodcurdling scream you can imagine. I opened the door to see the young man pinned to the ground, looking very pale and shaking as he regained consciousness. Unfortunately, mother-in-law was straddling him (heaven knows how she managed that position) and rubbing his groin.

For all the world, she had the look of a pile of clothes that needed ironing bouncing up and down like a pogo stick on amphetamines. She took some pulling off let me tell you – I now know how the term 'scared stiff' got its name. You see, even though the lad was now free of the pogo stick, he lay on the floor as rigid as a plank, arms outstretched for his mother, eyeballs bulging as if he was about to give birth at any second.

Come to think of it, if I hadn't got into the room when I did, he might just have (unwillingly) succeeded in confounding medical science in pushing the bounds of conception beyond its natural state.

My timely reminder of the incident concerning her mother's little indiscretion worked a treat and she gave in – but only on the condition that we stayed in a place called *Le Petit Nid D'amour*. Now I am the first to admit that my French leaves a lot to be desired, but when I said to her that 'The Little Soldier' was a strange name for a hotel, she made no attempt whatsoever to correct me, and I could've sworn that the right side of her top lip curled in the way that it does when she's got one over on me.

Well, it turns out I was right. As far as I was concerned we had booked in to a budget 'hotel' with bed, a pillow each and ensuite (soap, towels and hot water optional at additional cost). Just the job as far as I was concerned. It was only when the confirmation arrived I realised to my horror we were staying in the place called *'The Little Love Nest'*. I tell you, Reg, I must brush up on my French. It was now clear to me (and the calendar confirmed the all too familiar date of the Queen's birthday ringed in red) that Maud was planning to make a romantic weekend of it.

Worse than that, when I read the confirmation again (and just before Maude snatched it away saying it had nothing to do with me), I saw that she'd booked the 'nuit de luxure' room with a four-poster bed, feature fireplace and bearskin rug. Any guesses what *'nuit de luxure'* means? Luxury? No...

Any other guesses? Never mind, I'll put you out of your misery It actually translates as *night of lust!*

Lust for the love of God! Four-poster beds, bearskin rugs. It confirmed to me that the women had gone mad, absolutely bonkers. I have my suspicions that she's been reading that *'50 Spades in May'* book, or whatever it's called that the world and his mother has been talking about. In any event, she can keep her fantasies to herself and I'll keep my dibber tucked away in a safe place.

...Anyway, as far as fancy old wooden beds go, I can't be doing with all that death-watch beetle, creaking joints and bed drapes designed to give a fruit bat claustrophobia.

Nevertheless, since the woman had been suckered into a pay upfront with a 'no refund special deal', I decided to abandon my principles in favour of saving the bank balance. However, I did take the precaution of packing my extra thick onesie with buttons designed to foil the Great Train robbers, plus an ample supply of Kevlar reinforced earplugs.

Determined to stand my ground on a second drawback of having to take the mother-in-law with us, I put my foot down on what I was prepared to allow mother-in-law to eat or drink in public.

To my surprise a rather flushed Maude (her French is better than mine) readily agreed on the list of banned substances, which included:

1.   **No sprouts**, since these make her fart for England. You may recall her getting Eric's Labrador into trouble when she let rip at Jack's

funeral. I know that the dog's mistake was making off to hide under Jack's coffin stand, but then it had just taken a face full of mother-in-law's noxious gases. In any event, I still thought it unfair that it got chucked out of the pub.

2.   **No salted peanuts** because I am fed up of being splattered with the regurgitated remains of, as Maude puts it, 'mothers little treat' as she gags on the bloody things.

3.   **No table wine or other alcohol** since this brings the very worst out in the old bat. One glass and she starts singing, then arguing, then fighting (or if it's a man, groping).

Once we had the menus organised, Maude moved on to what clothes I was to be allowed to wear. She says my beige suit was completely out of the question, since light coloured trousers are not something men of my age should be wearing.

As if to press the point, she said that she was not prepared to guard my back again while I stood in front of a radiator to let my wet patch evaporate. I should explain she was referring to the little accident I had in the men's toilets at that local council presentation on global warming.

I have to say the only warming I felt that night was a groin on fire from Maude pushing me onto a radiator while I dried myself out, since she said I hadn't been standing close enough, it was talking too long and people were becoming curious as to why there was steam coming out of my ears.

At least it kept me warm once the pain subsided. Which was useful since it took ages to get home through that snow storm, which you will remember was quite peculiar for a late June evening. Nevertheless, Maude refuses to believe that 'my little accident', as she constantly refers to it, was due to that terror all men dread – the high pressure tap that splashes water over your trousers, when all you're trying to do is wash your hands.

I suspect she trots out this little line as a means of control, since, in common with all women, she knows how to get under a man's skin by tapping into our innermost fears, aka, UTVD (upper thigh visual dampness). Things went from bad to worse when I thought she said I had to wear a mourning suit. When I said it would be quite apt to wear a mourning suit, she gave me a look of contempt and said that saying such things was bad luck for weddings, and that I knew full well she had meant a morning suit.

As far as I'm concerned, Reg, the only bad luck about weddings is being made to go to them. As you would expect, I had a ready-made reply. However, the 'don't you dare say it' look she shot me encouraged me to retreat to the shed.

The microwave's just dinged, Reg, …will be back with you in a tick…

***

Who needs to watch that '30 Minute Meals' bloke on telly when you can get from freezer to fork in less than four minutes? Why am I microwaving my own lunch again you might ask? Well, all I said to Maude was, "We need some dish washer tablets, would you like me to take you shopping."

Simple enough statement wouldn't you think? Not if you're Maude. She accused me of wanting her out of the house because I couldn't possibly know whether we needed dishwasher tablets, since I never went near the machine.

Her accusation was a gross exaggeration, and you will know from our monthly get together to compare wood drill bits that I have, more than once, taken a couple of mugs out of the machine to make us a drink of tea.

I'll admit that I'm reluctant to load the dishwasher since every time I do, I get told off for placing stuff in the wrong order, or on the wrong shelf or wrong something else. What's a man to do? Well, when I was looking under the sink this morning for something to clean one of the gutters out, I happened to notice Maude only had two dishwasher tablets left because the tin fell on me. Hence my constructive offer to take the woman shopping.

Now a cynic may think that my sole aim was to distract her from discovering I had, in fact, taken what I later discovered to be one of her new table napkins to clean out the gutter, when in all innocence, I thought it was just a piece of old cloth.

It would have been pure coincidence, let me tell you, that if, in wandering around the supermarket, I had come across a replacement napkin while Maude was doing whatever women do in bloody supermarkets.

In any event, my plan failed miserably. As only Maude can, she discovered the missing napkin, suggested what I could do with the gutter, which I can tell you didn't involve rain, and flounced out of the house with her shopping bags shouting "...and make sure you clean the microwave after you've used it."

...Anyway, on with the wedding.

Having spent the best part of an hour cleaning the car ready for Maude, the mother-in-law and their fascinators, I made the mistake of leaving one of the windows open. In my mind this made sense so that I could give the car a good airing and head off any accusation that the car still smelled of grass clippings (how does the woman think the stuff gets to the waste dump – the grass fairy?).

It wasn't until I loaded the car with enough suitcases for a trek across the Antarctic and opened the door for the two women in my life, that I realised something was very wrong. That old music hall joke that goes something like...

I know *what* it is.

I know *who* did it

I don't know *where* it is

...came to mind as Maude reeled from the pong, poked me in the ribs with her favourite pointy finger and told me she wasn't prepared to step foot into the car until I found it, got rid of it, then sanitised the car.

At least the mother-in-law wasn't bothered since she lost her sense of smell years ago and was all for clambering into the backseat. When Maude went to pull her out again, the old girl instinctively clasped her handbag to her chest.

What she didn't know was that Maude had already found the stash of salted peanuts and 'just in case' condom her mother thought she had hidden. Ah well, ignorance is bliss, eh? Just then, next door's cat shot from under one of the car seats and bolted, taking full advantage of the mother-in-law's wide gate as it shot between her legs and disappeared into number 36's *Delphiniums.*

It took 30 sodding minutes to clean that car out. Granted, half of that was spent convincing Maude that her carriage was now in a fit state to carry her. Just as we were all getting into the car, the fool over the fence stuck his head over the divide that maintains our uneasy peace. I couldn't resist giving him a piece of my mind.

"Do you know your cat has just crept in, crapped, and crept out of my car?"

"How do you know it was my cat?" he replied.

"How many other cats do you know that are cross eyed, sport a nose stud and have 'love, hate' tattooed across their front paws?"

The idiot replied that it was cruel of me to have thrown water at the cat, to which I responded that it wasn't particularly polite for the cat to dump in my car and would he like to clean it out.

Just as he opened his mouth to make another stupid remark, he fell off the bin he'd been standing on, and from the language coming out of him as he hit the ground, I can only surmise that he landed in the cat crap I'd thrown back over the fence.

"Game set and match," I said to Maude as we pulled out of the drive. For once she seemed to be in total agreement with me, which I saw as rather curious, but then she did seem peculiarly distracted look in her eyes.

And so began our weekend away. The wife spent her time reading that gardening book I was telling you about, and from what I could see, the mother-in-law became increasingly agitated as she continuously peered into her handbag, between shooting me an accusing glance as our eyes met in the mirror.

***

The two-hour journey to the Frenchified hotel was uneventful which, looking back on what was to follow, had the effect of lulling me into a false sense of security. As we pulled into the car park of the *Le Petit Nid D'amour*, it struck me that the place was about as French as the croissants we get in our local greasy spoon.

I suppose the giveaway was the 'Patrons are kindly requested not to stub cigarettes out on the founder's bust' sign that was *blu-tacked* to the front door. Not something you would be likely to see outside the lobby of your average Parisian hotel, or 'otel' as the French say, Reg.

My impression of the place didn't improve as I 'dinged' the service bell at the reception desk (which sounded exactly like Maude's microwave, in front of which I would much preferred to have be standing.

Anyway, after what seemed like an age, a scruffy woman who said that she was the owner shuffled into sight wearing a tall woolly hat, finger mittens and suede leather ankle boots with fake fur edging. I have to say, Reg, the sight of her didn't fill me with confidence for the state of the heating system.

Attempting to make polite conversation as I filled in a form that required I tell my life story apart from my inside leg measurement (I blame Europe, you know), I tried my best to engage the woman with the red tipped nose in polite conversation – I should have known better.

"I'm interested to know where the French influence comes from," said I.

"French?"

"Oh, you mean the name of the place – that's down to my long -gone husband. I can't speak a word of the stuff and should change it all, I suppose."

Feeling just the slightest bit embarrassed I felt the need to apologise for my insensitivity – which, as you know, I am not known for.

"I'm so sorry for your loss, it must be really hard running a place like this on your own."

"Loss?" she replied in a quizzical sort of way. "No such luck. When I said long gone, what I meant was that he buggered off with a door-step onion seller called Aramis years ago – and good riddance to them I say. As for running this place, frying a bit of bacon every morning and changing the bed sheets every other week – nothing to it really."

At this point Maude began to look a little uneasy. I, on the other hand, really started to warm to this woman, and when she said her only inconvenience since her husband left was having to buy onions from the supermarket I thought, *she'll do for me.*

I like to think that she also started to take a shine to me, since it was clear that we were able to converse 'man-to-man' so to speak and she seemed genuinely interested on our reason for booking.

"What, do you mean St Martin's and vicar Vincent?" she said.

Maude chipped in to say she was sure that was the name of the church written on the invitation.

"Oh dear, well I'm sure everything will be fine and at least the weather forecast is good for tomorrow, apart from the sleet, that is."

When I asked her if there was a problem, here's how the conversation went...

"Well, it's just that he tends to get his words a little mixed up when he gets too relaxed."

"But how long has he been conducting wedding services at the church?"

"Well, it must be about 30 years now."

"Then it seems we should be in for an interesting time, because if he's not relaxed by now, he never will be."

"Well, he will be if he has a drink," she said without raising her eyes from the reception desk as she scanned the registration form on which I had just finished writing my memoir.

"I do hope you enjoy your stay (it was now as though she was reading from a script). Breakfast is served between 8 and 9, and the hot water goes on between 7.15 and 8am."

With that, she handed over the key (which weighed a ton on account of it being attached to a 6" x 1" lump of lead as an anti-theft device) and shuffled back down the corridor rubbing her hands together and blowing on them.

I could tell how cold it was from her breath condensing as it hit the air; that and the thermometer on the wall, which seemed to be shivering. On reflection, this probably had more to do with the railway line, which, from the sound of it, ran straight through the lounge of her little hideaway. Well done, Maude, I thought.

The French letters (no pun intended) on the door turned out to be the only foreign influence that the room displayed. The walls and ceilings were decorated in mock Tudor panelling that gave the impression of being entombed in a packing crate.

Not that you could see much of walls or ceilings since most of the space was taken up by that bloody four-poster bed. You should've seen Maude's eyes light up when she caught sight of it. In contrast I closed mine and thought about the tool box I was halfway through building in the garage. It seemed to do the trick because in my mind's eye I was seeing dovetail joints, rather than aching joints.

At least the adjoining door that we booked was in working order and meant I could install the mother-in-law in her room – and keep an eye on what she was up to. Which, I'm pleased to say, turned out to be not very much since the car journey seemed to have knocked her out and she slept for the rest of the afternoon.

This despite me poking her quite hard on occasion just to check she was still breathing – you know, the kind of thing you do when you have your first child. Well, what goes around, comes around, don't you think, Reg...

Now it's only because you're my best mate, Reg, that I'm going to share with you what happened next, since it involves intimate doings that men of our age shouldn't have to put up with. As you know, Maude doesn't drink spirits as a rule – and I know to scarper any time I do see her drink. Well, this time there was nowhere to scarper to. As the evening wore on she started to sway and smile at me a lot – which I thought was wind at first, until she began to wink at me with all the charm of a pantomime cow.

At least I had the mother-in-law under control – or so I thought. She believed she was drinking neat vodka. She was actually drinking iced water and, apart from a remarkable placebo effect that involved a lot of hiccupping and out of tune humming of *Devil Women*, she remained well-behaved and busied herself stroking the hotel's stuffed cat, which had been minding its own business to one side of a roaring fire. So far so good you might think.

Indeed, had it not been for the hotel owner's real cat showing up, things would have remained that way. However, the cat that could actually walk and meow made the mistake of jumping onto the mother-in-law's left shoulder from behind.

Thinking the animal was about to attack her new-found friend, the old woman made a grab for the now hissing animal, which resulted in the thing swiping her cheek with its claws.

Moving with more speed than I've seen for years, she sprang to her feet to shoo the offending cat out of the bar, while at the same time flinging the stuffed cat in the other direction and urging it to take cover. Unfortunately, the other direction was straight onto that roaring fire I mentioned.

I have to say the hotel owner was very good about it, and said she only bought the cat from a taxidermist as a reminder of her husband, after he ran away with that onion seller. When I asked what it was about the specimen that the reminded her of her husband she said...

"Ginger hair, sly, and he never moved a muscle in his waking hours."

Anyway, Maude broke the tension by telling me to get the mother-in-law back to her room and settled for the night – and why I was at it, to check the thermostat in *our* room so that it was, as she put it 'nice and warm'.

Normally I would have objected but given the tense atmosphere in the bar and the nauseating smell of burning cat's fur and formaldehyde, I was ready for a change of scene.

Having settled the mother-in-law down, I shut the connecting door and as instructed, checked the room thermostat. I thought it odd that, although it was reading 'high heat', the radiator was stone cold.

I know you're going to say I should have minded my own business, but since it is my habit to carry a radiator bleed key, I thought I was doing the hotel owner a favour by fixing the problem. Unfortunately, it took rather more force than I anticipated to turn the key, with the result that the radiator water plug came out in my hands. On the plus side this at least allowed all of the air to escape.

On the downside it allowed a torrent of boiling water to shoot out of the radiator. By the time I got that bloody plug back in, the tips of my fingers were red raw and throbbing so hard I thought they were going to explode.

I tell you all of this by way of explaining how I came to find Maude's naughty book. I thought it was a piece of old cloth that was stuffed behind the radiator, and which I grabbed by way of drying my hands and take my mind off the pain.

In fact, she had wrapped that gardening book I was telling you about in a piece of chamois leather. It wasn't until I unwrapped the chamois that I realised it wasn't a gardening book at all.

It took a page or two before I realised what I was reading since inexplicably, the front and back cover of the book had been removed –

strange don't you think? Anyway, as soon as it dawned on me what she'd been reading, all her little hints and insistence on a four-poster bed clicked into place.

By way of protecting myself I did a quick rummage of our suitcases to check that there weren't any handcuffs, leather thongs or suchlike to be found and gave a sigh of relief, though I did find one of those battery candles I mentioned. I assumed Maude had just bought an extra wedding present for the happy couple.

Leaving nothing to chance, I decided that it was necessary to suffer an unexpected attack of sciatica and re-entered the bar with an exaggerated limp, rubbed my left buttock vigorously, and gave Maude my Best Man-flu type of look.

Much good it did me since Maude was too far gone to notice anything other than what she thought was a bulge in my trousers. Reg, even you would have been frightened by the look in her eyes. It then dawned on me I'd made the mistake of stuffing the chamois leather into my trouser pocket.

Realising I couldn't put the moment off any longer, I helped Maude stagger up the stairs and just managed to get into the room before my faked sciatica turned into the real thing. Incredibly, as soon as she caught sight of that bloody bed again, she seemed to revive and dashed into the bathroom.

You'd have been proud of my turn of speed in getting my clothes off, thick onesie on, and into bed with the eiderdown wrapped so tightly around me that I was finding it difficult to breathe.

After what seemed an eternity (it was like waiting to be shot), Maude re-entered the bedroom humming that stupid *Devil Woman* song like her mother. I tell you, Reg, that *Cliff Richard* has got a lot to answer for.

The one saving grace was that I'd taken particular care to turn the lights out. As Maude went to climb into bed, she stubbed her big toe on one of the legs, which had the pleasing effect of stopping that bloody song and keeping her occupied for a few minutes while I tightened my grip on the eiderdown.

Unfortunately, all too soon she regained her state of semi-consciousness and started all that blowing in the ear and stroking of the neck malarkey. I reminded her about my sciatica attack and that it was now very stiff indeed. This just seemed to encourage the stupid woman even more.

"Why did you turn off all the lights," said Maude.

"We always turn the lights off – remember you said on our honeymoon that you were shy."

"But that was 45 years ago."

"And I've lived every minute of it."

"What did you say?"

"I said I've loved every minute, my dear."

Not to be deterred, Maude pulled at the eiderdown, dragging me into the middle of the bed with it. For a few minutes her hands were all over me, and I could sense that before long she would find a way of penetrating my flock shield.

It was then I realised I could feel two more hands than was natural. First three, then four – and that wasn't including mine. Not only that, I could feel two boobs pressing into my chin – and two into the nape of my neck.

Now I'm no prude, Reg, and I'm sure in our younger days the thought of a three in a bed romp would have seemed most appealing. But that was then, and this was now. It was all I could do to let out a 'what the feck...' as I tried to make sense of things.

Had the woman been so overcome by reading that bloody book that she'd done some perverse deal in the bar while I was getting away from the barbecued cat? A nanosecond after I screamed, Maude screamed.

The mother-in-law gave a gummy grin as she lit her face from under her chin with a small torch she'd found somewhere, and which made her look like a pumpkin on Halloween night. Yuck...

If nothing else, I'd inadvertently discovered a sure-fire way of sobering someone up who's half-cut. Maude shot out of bed and hopped around to my side (no small feat for a big woman) rubbing her swollen big toe in one hand, while grabbing onto the bed frame with the other. In contrast, the mother-in-law seemed quite happy lying where she was, and wasn't for moving.

It seems she too had a soft spot for four-poster beds, though what she was thinking of when she climbed in with us I simply don't want to contemplate. The shock having done its job in sobering Maude up, you can imagine I paid the price once she got her mother back into her own room, since I got the blame for not locking the interconnecting door earlier in the evening.

What the hell, Reg; mistake or not, it got me out of a bloody tight spot and into a good night's kip, courtesy of those Kevlar earplugs. Breakfast started off very quietly with Maude's eyes darting between me and the mother-in-law who, to my surprise, still had flushed cheeks and seemed distracted by obsessing on a banana.

I noticed, or to be more precise, heard, Maude's foot tapping on the mock parquet flooring. Now you have seen Maude do this before, so you know it only meant one thing – trouble ahead. Sure enough before long she shouted at her mother, "Are you going to eat that thing, or what?" The old girl wasn't paying any attention to her daughter. I noticed she was looking over my shoulder at an elderly man on the next table. Intrigued, I looked back at her, only to see her winking at the poor sod, before purposely peeling the banana and sliding it almost whole into her gummy mouth.

You know, Reg, I was slightly in awe that she could manage such a feat at her age. Then I heard the old bloke gagging and I turned around to see a waiter attempting the Heimlich Manoeuvre to dislodge a length of Cumberland sausage from his throat.

It seemed the two of them had been giving each other the eye and competing to see who could slide the most into their mouths, most provocatively, without choking. Well, as you would expect, mother-in-law won, and all the silly sod got for his trouble was bruised ribs, sore throat and a good telling off from his wife for being so disgusting.

As the man's colour slowly changed from blue to beetroot red, his wife glowered at the mother-in-law. In an act of defiance which I admired, Maude's mother gave the woman the most innocent smile you could imagine while giving the banana another exaggerated suck.

It was with some relief that the head waiter asked us to leave the restaurant, which you will be pleased to know we complied with great dignity, a mushy banana, and the moral high ground as we watched the old bloke spit out the last of the Cumberland sausage, which, with good aim, landed in his wife's coffee. My last word on the subject, which I know you will agree is a sombre testament to the institution of marriage, is that his wife was far more concerned with the coffee stains on her blouse, than for her husband as he gasped for air, before retrieving the lump of sausage by way of finishing off his breakfast.

...Will need to email you back, Reg. It seems Maude is in need of my pest control skills.

***

Do you know, Reg, for someone who can wield a spade with more force than your average TV celebrity gardener, Maude is peculiarly squeamish about slugs. So, every time she comes across one of the beasties, instead of despatching it herself, I suddenly become husband of the month.

Never mind, I do get the greatest satisfaction from lobbing them into the fool over the fence's garden, then listening to his cries of anguish as he complains to his wife about yet another infestation that have done for his Hostas.

Anyway, enough of gardening and on with the wedding. We arrived in time for the 'pre-wedding drinks reception' (Trevor's wife had clearly been watching too many of those TV celebrity weddings) to be greeted by the man himself with the clueless Cleo on his arm who was looking slightly the worse for wear.

I say worse for wear. The giveaway was that between hiccups, she kept blowing with the side of her mouth on an artificial daisy, which was dangling limply from its broken plastic stem on her fascinator.

To be honest I thought her pale complexion was caused by the women hyperventilating keeping the daisy from irritating her nose (which you will remember is not one of her more diminutive features). Then again, I don't suppose the glass of bubbly in each hand helped.

Trevor's opening gambit was as predictable as it was inane.

"…Pleased that you could prise yourself away from your shed," he said, to which I couldn't help myself by responding…

"Not even my new workshop vacuum cleaner would have kept me away, Trevor."

Mention of the vacuum cleaner caused the clueless Cleo to blush.

"Speaking of which," I added, "who would have thought that an electric motor connected to a suction hose would bring us all together here today."

You guessed it. That earned me a dig from Maude's finger. Cleo's neck turned red and I thought she was going to pass out as she gave an extra strong blow on the dangling daisy.

"Is that the time," Cleo commented in a breathy sort of way. With that she dragged Trevor away saying that they needed to practice their final positions again. For a moment, Reg, I thought the mention of a vacuum cleaner had raised her passions once again, and that she was talking about something she may have read in the *Kama Sutra*.

Maude gave me a death stare and told me to get her mother off the organist's lap and check that the man didn't want to press charges. Having calmed the organist down and assured him that a visit to the STI clinic would not be necessary, I noticed the vicar standing at the bar.

Clearly the worse for wear, he had a line of drinks in front of him, purchased, presumably, by guests trying to buy their way into heaven. As time went on, the vicar started to bless everything that moved and some that didn't, including a fruit machine and a stuffed bear, which had apparently occupied the same position for over 100 years.

The bear didn't say anything. The slot machine played him a tune and asked him to put another coin in the slot. "My son," said the vicar in a rather commanding, if slightly slurred, voice. "It is for you to give to the church and it is my job to administer sucker."

Then he blessed the machine, which didn't answer. A rather elegant lady sat next to the fruit machine misheard the vicar, told him to stop being disgusting and lobbed a box of confetti she was holding at him. Remarkably he saw it coming, ducked and made a swift exit.

The same couldn't be said for the other men in the bar, who were sulking over ruined pints full of bits of coloured paper. As the box hit the fake Victorian fan hanging overhead, it turned the confetti into a veritable snowstorm.

***

Taking our seats in the church was something of an anti-climax after the entertainment in the bar, or so I thought. All seemed ready. The Groom stood nervously next to his Best Man, who seemed even more nervous as he went through the time-honoured ritual of checking every pocket he possessed several times to make sure he still had the rings.

The Bride's family glared at the Groom's family who glared back, as each tried to estimate who was better represented, how many of the women were wearing the same frocks, and who had the tallest fascinator.

Now and then you could catch sight of the photographer darting from pillar to pillar, trying to remain inconspicuous, but instead looking like a very badly trained private investigator as he took shot after shot of anything that moved, including a dove, which, as it turned out, was meant to have been released when the married couple left the church for photographs.

Instead, a little sod aged about nine opened the cage, releasing the terrified bird, which shot straight up into the rafters and relieved its stress by crapping on everything immediately below it. Believe me, you've never seen so many fascinators removed from hair extensions so quickly in all your life.

Anyway, opening every door in sight and a well-aimed shoe dislodged the now much lighter dove as it saw the light, so to speak, and shot out of the church as if it had a peregrine falcon up its arse. Calm once more restored, the vicar took up his position and smiled inanely at the congregation as he gently swayed from side to side.

After a minute or two, and becoming conscious that nothing was happening, the vicar looked behind him to see where the organist had got to. Realising the man was missing and seeing the Bride waiting nervously at the back of the church, he decided to take things into his own hands. Trotting to one side of the church like a geisha, he picked up a DVD that lay on a side table and inserted it into the player.

Trotting back to the centre of the aisle looking very pleased with himself, he, we, and more particularly the Bride and Trevor, waited for the music to begin. Unfortunately, instead of *Wagner's Bridal Chorus*, 'We Plough the Fields and Scatter' boomed out of the speakers.

I genuinely don't know who was more surprised, the Bride, Groom or the organist who had now popped his head around the vestry door and seemed to be looking to see where the mother-in-law was seated.

Judging by the way he hobbled over to the organ loft, I suspected he was late due to his need to apply a soothing balm to his men's bits, following the mauling he got from the Maude's mother. Safely seated (though I did notice it took three of four attempts before he put his full weight on the seat), the organist gave the sort of cough that all boys of a certain age give at their school medical to check that everything that should have dropped by the age of 15, had dropped.

In any event, seeing the organist was in position, the vicar stopped singing along to the Harvest Festival hymn and ejected the disc from the machine.

With that, the organist struck up with an absolutely splendid rendition of Here Comes the Bride. I noticed, however, that Trevor looked a little dishevelled and pink around the gills and pondered whether my mention of the vacuum cleaner in the bar had set the seemingly not so clueless, Cleo, off again.

Of course, I had to hope Maude hadn't made the same connection or she'd be after one of those modern cyclone versions, what with the Queen's birthday coming up and all, the last thing I needed was a turbo boost of any kind.

Anyway, as the Bride-to-be reached her position, the wedding photographer went in for a close-up shot. At this point it was clear the vicar was, indeed, the worse for wear because he pushed the Groom to one side and bodily pulled the photographer centre stage, telling him to hold hands with his 'sweetheart'. It was at this point the congregation gasped and Trevor's daughter let out a shriek.

"Don't be nervous, my dear, here he is," announced the vicar with a cheery smile.

"But it's the wrong man," she said.

The vicar took a step back, glared at the still confused photographer and said,

"Imposter, what are you doing here; who are you?"

"I'm the photographer."

"Then be gone," replied the vicar, before finishing with a flourish, "and you're a clicking disgrace to your profession."

The amount of alcohol the vicar had consumed in the bar was clearly beginning to have an effect, and the prophetic words of the hotel owner were about to come home to roost.

The Bride and real Groom smiled nervously at one another, held hands and looked intently at the vicar. For his part, the vicar opened his eyes from several moments of internal reflection, or sleep. His body seem to physically relax as he dropped his shoulders and started to smile at the two of them with the strangest of expressions.

Since I know that what I'm about to tell you will sound so far-fetched as to be taken from a BBC current affairs programme, I think the easiest thing to do is to relate to you, word for word, what happened next. And so, in the words of the vicar...

"Bearly Deloved, we have come together in the gresence of Pod, to witness the marriage of Jobert and Rane."

For the second time, Reg, there was an audible gasp from the congregation, which left the vicar looking a little bemused. The Groom leant forward with, I must say, great tact and said:

"It's *Jane*, vicar,"

"That's what I said, dear boy, that's what I said. Don't worry, you're just perverse – I mean nervous," replied the vicar.

The Bride and Groom looked at each other in a sort of daze. Nevertheless, the vicar continued without flinching.

"The Bible teaches us that garriage is a mift and a means of his grace, a moly hystery in which man and woman become one flesh.

"It is Pod's gurpose that, as wusband and hife they give themselves to each other."

By this time the congregation was all out of gasps, and so resorted to dropping their lower jaws slightly and scrunching their eyes in a sort of *is this really happening* sort of way.

Still the vicar continued with even more of a flourish as he got into his stride...

"This is the way of life, created and hallowed gy Bod, that Jobert and Rane are now to begin; they will now join hands and exchange volemn sows."

Now swaying more noticeably, the vicar offered...

"Now, mepeat after re...

"I, Jobert , take you, Rane, to be wy fife, from this fay dorward, in hickness and in sealth, till peath us do dart."

Now I know you won't believe me, but 'Jobert' did exactly as he was instructed – before the vicar interrupted him and chided the young man for not speaking properly or taking the wedding service seriously.

As the service progressed, the organist began to look more and more nervous, and took several sips from a hip flask before striking up with a hymn that was much too modern for my liking. Would you believe some people started clapping in time to the music, then holding both arms above their heads and smiling inanely at the ceiling – most odd.

This seemed to take the vicar by surprise and he stopped swaying momentarily before looking up to the ceiling to see what some of the congregation were looking at, then glancing over his shoulder at the organist who *was* swaying. Not wanting to be outdone, I suppose, the vicar then encouraged everyone to join in like a cheerleader at a football match.

After a sermon that defied any sane person to follow it, and watching the organist take several more swigs from his hip flask, rings were exchanged, and the vicar announced with the satisfaction of a job well done:

"I now pronounce you wan and mife."

Clearly having had enough, the Groom leant toward the vicar in a more menacing tone than previously, and said:

"You mean man and wife, vicar."

"That's what I said, dear boy, that's what I said. No need to be nervous now; you're spliced and have your honeymoon to look forward to," replied the vicar winking at the Groom with both eyes (which means it was a blink, doesn't it?) almost losing his balance as he lost sight of the horizon.

Quite sensibly, the Bride and Groom looked at each other, shrugged their shoulders and walked down the aisle to a rousing rendition of *The Wedding March* that included just one or two bum notes, which I put down to the organist's hip flask.

As Maude pushed me into the aisle and out of the church, I looked back to see the vicar sat next to the communion table finishing off the wine while talking to the lectern, which didn't answer back. As the vicar placed the now empty communion cup upside down on an altar candle by way of extinguishing it, he caught sight of the photographer who was taking some general shots of the stained glass windows in the transept.

"No photographs, bloody press, I wasn't there I tell you, now sod off and go clean your lens," shouted the vicar before raising his eyes to the ceiling, hiccupping, and asking forgiveness for swearing in church.

The photographer ran for it while he still could. He only stopped running when the woman I had seen him with earlier in the day grabbed his arm and told him to pull himself together. Fortunately, she had set the photographic paraphernalia up outside the church ready for the torture that was the wedding group photographs. It turned out that it was his first wedding assignment, and the woman with him was a sort of mentor, if only to stop him running away.

Despite this, each photograph took a lifetime because he kept checking his camera, then lighting, then back to his camera, which was no fun since it had started to sleet.

As the photographer became more nervous, he barked his instructions ever louder, and at one point, I thought he was going to blow his bulb so to speak, when a little oik with a cardboard lucky horseshoe kept shoving it up the Maid of Honour's dress.

As you can imagine, she was not best pleased with. Not least because him hiking her dress up revealed a packet of cigarettes clamped to her thigh with a rather delicate blue garter – or so I was told.

Things didn't get any better as both sides of the family started to look accusingly at each other, each believing the other was having more photographs taken of them with the Bride and Groom. I have to say the 'mothers' were by far the worst offenders as they tried to push each other out of the way, vying for prime photographic position.

After about 20 minutes of kids pulling tongues at the camera and the vicar blessing anything in sight, swigging from the organist's hip flask, and picking shards of candle wax off his cassock, everyone had had enough and headed back to the bar.

At the same time, I noticed the peculiar sight of the organist running across the graveyard while waving a broken candle above his head screaming, "Sod the vicar; I know where the skeletons were buried." Somehow, Reg, I don't think he was talking about the ones he was treading all over. Anyway, it was a relief to get out of the sleet and back into the bar, which by now had been cleared of most of the confetti, save for a few flakes on the stuffed bear's snout and right eyebrow – which I thought gave it a rather jaunty and up-to-date look.

Not long after, the master of ceremonies ordered us upstairs to meet the Bride and Groom. In my mind, Reg, this was a waste of drinking time since I'd already met them. So, there we were, lined up as if waiting to be called into the headmaster's office, thinking of something original to say to the happy couple.

Then again, I suppose the new Mr and Mrs were thinking much the same thing as they greeted so many strangers, while racking their brains as to who the hell they were shaking hands with, and who invited them anyway.

It was one such look that the Groom gave Maude's mother. Never backwards at coming forward, the old girl launched herself at the poor sod, sucked his lips by way of a slobbery type of kiss and thrust her right hand into his groin.

Full marks to the guy for manning-up as he mostly managed to disguise the little jump he gave as a natural reaction to having his plums felt by a stranger. He let out only the tiniest of whimpers. The Bride looked at the Groom, the Groom looked at the knobbly hand between his legs, and I made for the bar.

Relief came when the apprentice photographer, who was still being shadowed by his minder, attempted to take some atmospheric close-up shots of the bridal cupcakes, if you know what I mean. At that very moment, a child's hand (which, judging by its girth, indicated that whatever it was attached to would do well to spend its school holidays at fat camp) emerged from under the table like something out of an *Alfred Hitchcock* movie, rummaged around for a few seconds before making contact with 250 calories, then withdrew like an octopus dragging its prey to the depths before devouring it.

Not unreasonably, this caused the now even more nervous photographer to recoil in fright, and in so doing, fall flat on his back. Unfortunately, he was still attached to the tablecloth he had grabbed in a vain effort to steady himself, which in turn, was still attached to a dozen cupcakes topped off with a less than convincing marzipan montage of the Bride and Groom, peel of wedding bells and a rather tacky plastic miniature vacuum cleaner.

While feeling just a little sorry for the photographer, at least everyone's eyes were on him (except for the Groom, whose eyes were still fixed on his groin) instead of the mother-in-law who by now had been whisked into the ladies restroom by Maude.

"At least he'll have got some good shots of the cupcakes in mid-air, don't you think?" said a bloke stood next to me at the bar.

"Well, Trevor wanted atmospheric – he got atmospheric, and I'm sure Cleo will soon whip those cupcakes into an *Eton Mess*. She never was one to waste anything," I replied.

"Except her time on Trevor, I suppose," my drinking companion replied as I warmed to the stranger who clearly had a well-developed intellect and keen sense of observation. With that, we both took a second swig of our pint and spent the rest of our time together talking about the merits of engineered wood versus laminate strip flooring.

Clueless Cleo had done that modern thing they do at weddings nowadays by mixing up family members on different tables, so they were forced to spend two hours together not talking, At least not beyond the banal:

1. "It's a lovely day for it."

2. "Didn't the Bride look lovely?"

3. "Shame about the weather."

4. "Did you see what the organist tried to do to the vicar with that candle?"

Fair enough, the last one wasn't run-of-the-mill for your average marriage ceremony – unless, I guess, you pay extra for the entertainment value and by way of the church raising money for its roof lead replacement fund.

Anyway, at least it broke the ice and meant the time we each spent rearranging our knives and forks and checking our mobile phones for messages that weren't there, was kept to a minimum.

It wasn't long before the food arrived, whereupon the mother-in-law's mood immediately darkened as she realised she wasn't getting the roast dinner she'd been expecting. Instead, we made sure she got mashed spuds and pureed carrots.

Unfortunately, as the rest of us tucked in to a nice piece of silver side, the mother-in-law succeeded in distracting the young man next to her by dropping a fork and asking the gullible pup to pick it up. As soon as he disappeared beneath the table, she pinched his sprouts, stuffed them into her gob and sucked them to death before Maude or I had chance to stop her.

As expected, within a few minutes, the old girl started to let go with a choreographed selection of farts, which included in the space of a 90-second rendition:

1.   **Silent but Deadly**: I don't think this requires any further explanation.

2.   **The Squeezebox**: announced by her jumping up a little as she pursed her cheeks to exact maximum force.

3.   **Rumble in the Jungle**: a resinous bass note that I've seen shake teacups off their saucers before now.

4.   **The Squealing Pig**: an extremely high-pitched fart that I have still to work out how she manages without the aid of a concealed dog whistle or rapidly deflating balloon.

Now had we been at a circus, I'm sure she would have got a round of applause, since even I had to admit there was a certain level of expertise being demonstrated. However, along with the sound effects came the smell.

Well, besides the sprouts, I don't know whether the grotesque source of her emanations had anything to do with her age, gender or general outlook on life, but I tell you this, there are those things in nature that are a natural phenomenon, and then there are my mother-in-law's farts.

To cap it all, knowing what was coming and the timing thereof, the mother-in-law looked intently at the young man as her poisonous wind made its presence known, and gave him a gummy smile in a 'there, there, bless' sort of way.

As you would expect, the young man started to blush thinking that he was being blamed for the stink. Attempting to go to his aid by way of explaining the mother-in-law's 'little problem', I was foiled by Maude jabbing me in the thigh with her fork.

I thought this was both sly and a little too hard for me to consider it a mild reprimand in daring to dob her mother in. Nevertheless, this was one of those occasions when I was proud to be British since the bulldog spirit cut in and everyone tucked in to the meal, while gagging quietly so as not to upset their table companions.

I say everyone. That is, of course, except the mother-in-law who was wearing a superior look as she pushed her still full plate of mashed potato and pureed carrots away, folded her arms and waited for the Spotted Dick to arrive.

Well, it certainly proves the point that you don't smell your own farts.

***

Apologies for the abrupt interruption to the email, Reg. You can tell its local election time since blokes with shiny teeth and coloured shooting targets pinned to their jackets keep knocking on the door.

This time it was the 'I'll tell you anything you want to hear if you vote for me' party. It seems in return for my vote he will fix the roads, sort out antisocial behaviour in the village and keep his monthly travel claim down to four figures (he didn't say which four, though).

He bottled it when I said I was content with his promise to solve the global warming crises, but could he sort out next door's cat. It was only then that I saw the claw marks on the back of his hand.

Anyway, he went away quite happy when I said I fully intended to vote for a man of integrity, honesty and who worked hard for the community without thought of furthering his own agenda. So as you would expect, Reg. There isn't a chance in hell that I'll be voting for any of the sods.

Well, on with the wedding and if mother-in-law's farts weren't enough to put up with, next came the interminable wedding speeches – or should I say festival of crap clichés?

On droned Trevor...

"Marriage is like two horses pulling in different directions and then they learn to pull together...

"...Robert is like the son I never had."

As he said this it occurred to me that the latter wasn't strictly true, but the test was inconclusive due to a mix up with the blood tests, money having changed hands and his assertion that he was on a botanical expedition to Madeira (which is very strange since he doesn't know the difference between a lavender and a levada).

Then, to cap it all, he came up with the cliché of the century:

"Marriage is about loving each other enough to overlook your other half's little habits..."

I imagine he meant things like Maude:

...Grinding her teeth to dust in bed every night,

...Mucking around with the setting on my surround sound system,

...Waking up with a hot flush because her HRT patch has come off again, which then sticks to *my* arse – and which I blame fair and square for my man-boobs

...Moaning about my need to sharpen woodwork tools on the kitchen table

…Complaining about me spitting on the grandchildren's cuts and grazes when it's a proven fact that spittle contains an antiseptic agent (I read it somewhere).

Anyway, she won't let me do it since the fool over the fence complained I had infected his stupid son's hand over that unfortunate incident when he stuck it under the fence to retrieve his ball from my dahlias.

If you ask me, it was a trivial incident and he only caught a glancing blow from my hoe. And anyway, I thought it was a rat and if he hadn't been wearing those black gloves it wouldn't have happened in the first place.

The most entertaining part of the afternoon was the Best Man's speech, which made Trevor drain of colour when the lad said that one of his close relatives was about to join them – it turned out he was joking about the Groom's wallet seeing the light of day, and not a teenager contesting Trevor's visit to Madeira.

That said, I thought the Best Man went a bit far when he made the Bride's eyes fill up by saying that, of course, her new husband was fully committed to their marriage.

So far, so good, but her watery eyes turned into a torrent when he added:

"…And even more so now that he has weaned himself off those Internet dating sites, but that she shouldn't worry because it was only the men's ones, so it didn't count anyway."

Eventually she stopped crying and because he wimped out and finished with a long list of 'knock knock' jokes, everyone's attention fell to zero as their thoughts turned to the evening do.

Speaking of which, I have to be honest with you, Reg, and say that things didn't turn out as I would've wanted. In fact, the Bride and Groom's opening dance, which kicked off the evening, set the tone for what was to follow.

As is the fashion, it seems, these days, they strode confidently into the middle of the dance-floor looking intently into each other's eyes, which belied the fact that they had been living together for the previous seven years.

I suppose it was this familiarity that led them to the disastrous decision to do what every other newly married couple seem to do these days and try to imitate *Jennifer Grey* and *Patrick Swayze* in *Dirty Dancing*.

Unfortunately, neither of them had quite the physique to carry it off given his delicate stature and she being as my mother used to put it, 'big boned'.

Nevertheless, they seemed to be making a fist of it, that is, until she broke off, scurried around the side of the room before imitating that run-in scene from the film. With a sense of hope over reality, she leapt into the air and launched herself at her new husband's up stretched arms.

...Well, the lad did his best to hold her weight, but the combination of kilograms and forward motion meant he didn't stand a chance.

They both crashed into the chocolate fountain (another modern fad – whatever happened to lettuce sandwiches and Garibaldi biscuits?). This was not a pretty sight and I wouldn't like to have paid the drycleaners bill to get all that coco off her wedding dress.

I did my best to help the hapless couple, but all I got for my best efforts was a poke in the ribs with Maude's favourite finger as she accused me of trying to snog the Bride, her evidence for which, she said, was a ring of chocolate around my lips.

It didn't seem to occur to the stupid woman that the last thing on my mind was kissing an overweight chocolate log, while she was in the middle of giving her new husband a punch to the left ear by way of retribution for having ruined her moment.

To be fair, everyone else in the room did a really good job in stifling their laughs by means of synchronised coughing, the mass looking at watches and a coordinated picking up of all manner of imaginary paraphernalia from the floor.

As I wiped the last of the chocolate from my face and asked Maude to stop poking me, I noticed the mother-in-law sat on the vicar's lap in one of the darker corners of the room. Given the afternoon both of them had had, plus the fact that they were wearing identical fixed grins on their faces, I took the view that I should leave them alone, and that the exercise would do them good at their time of life.

It was at that point I thought the building was collapsing, when in fact it was only the DJ firing up the music – I call it 'music' in the loosest sense of the word.

You guessed it, the noise led to an immediate exodus as everyone over 65 made for the other room, where they could carry on with their quiet drink, exchanging tales of who had the most ailments and when their next hospital appointment was.

It wasn't long before the DJ became desperate (although why this should have been a surprise to him was a surprise to me) and, in desperation, resorted to playing *YMCA* and *the Birdie Song* to get any reaction at all from the brave souls that had remained in the room.

As the evening wore on, Maude started drinking once more and, staying clear of her as I thought about that bloody four-poster again, I watched her latch on to the Best Man as they attempted a head-banging dance to *Status Quo's 'Get Down, Deeper and Down'*. Unfortunately, because Maude suffers from vertigo, she soon overbalanced and fell into a dizzy heap pulling the Best Man onto her as he gallantly tried to help her to her feet.

Clearly the worse for wear for having drunk too many *'Panty Dropper'* cocktails, she tried to wrap her legs around the terrified boy shouting 'come to teacher' at the top of her voice.

Luckily, due to her being a little on the fleshy side, he bounced off again and sprang back to his feet in much the same way that a cat always lands right way up, then quickly made for the bar.

It was, therefore, left to me to retrieve the women, which, due to my years of experience and hours spent in my shed, I succeeded without falling into her clutches.

Hardly had I got Maude to her feet than there was a rumpus just behind us. It turned out that (in the best tradition of family weddings) two relatives had started to argue over some incident long lost in the mists of time, but about which each still held a grudge.

The shadow boxing and rather amateurish attempt at karate which followed was only interrupted by the photographer (who had seen sense and taken a drink) asserted his position and asked everybody to clap as he took the 'going away shot' of the Bride and Groom, which was peculiar since they were spending the night in the hotel.

Safe to say, the two men who had been arguing resumed their rather poor imitation of Bruce Lee's *'Enter The Dragon'* as soon as the newlyweds had made their dramatic exit from the room – into which they returned 10 minutes later to carry on drinking.

At this point, Reg, I'd had enough and decided (at some risk to myself, I might add) to get the mother-in-law off the vicar's lap and shove Maude into the car. Unfortunately, in one last attempt to thwart my best laid plans, the bloody DJ started to play '*Lady in Red*'.

Unluckily, this is Maude's favourite record and though drunk as a skunk, I could see that she was intent on grabbing me for one of those standing on the spot, turning around sort of dances, in which I had no intention of participating. In a moment of pure genius and taking full advantage of the fact that the mother-in-law was also full to the brim of sherry and endorphins from her escapade with the vicar, I pushed the two women together.

They spent the next five minutes nuzzling each other's neck (one nibbling, one sucking) in blissful ignorance of what they were up to. So, just to finish off letting you know what you missed, I attached a couple of photos we were sent a week or so later by Trevor, who asked us to pick which ones we'd like enlarged.

You will notice they demonstrate a certain lack of skill on the part of the photographer, and a further calculated insult from that stupid cousin of mine.

Despite how crap the bloody photos were, Maude went all gooey and said that she'd enjoyed the wedding so much (Lord knows how she remembered any of it) that she wanted to renew our wedding vows.

Renew our wedding vows – can you credit it?

She spends her life poking me in the ribs with that special sharpened finger of hers, telling me to get my woodworking tools off the dining table, and making me cook my own bloody chicken-ding meals – and now she wants to renew our sodding wedding vows.

Well, Reg, I squinted at Maude, then at the mother-in-law sat in her rocking chair (fantasising about that vicar judging by her flushed cheeks), sucking a melted chocolate bar she'd taken off the mantle shelf above the fire and thought...

...Maude being her mother's daughter, I'm off to the bloody shed.

END

4 The Crabby Old Git on Parenting

Dear Reg,

I thought you might like to know about the few hours I recently spent with my niece, Jane. You know, Tragic Trevor's daughter, and her new husband, Robert, after they got back from honeymoon at the M93 protest camp and spending a week in wellies, building tree houses and flying around on zip wires to keep one step ahead of the police.

This proved unsuccessfull as it turned out since they swapped free love for two nights at Her Majesty's pleasure – not literally you understand, honeymoon notwithstanding.

Anyway, I came across them in the village stocking up on herbal remedies before heading back to her parents and facing a grilling on the joys of honeymooning.

Now call me a cynic, but I don't think young Robert will be telling his new father-in-law about the mooning he got up to, which led to them being arrested in the first place. I've no time for Bobbies since they stopped calling me 'Sir' and started addressing me as 'mate' all the time.

But it can't have been a nice scene to look up into the tree tops at that camp and see Robert's bare cheeks yawning at you – and I don't mean the ones attached to his chops. It's enough to put anyone off their dinner – even police constables, and that's saying something from the number of times I've seen them parked up on double yellow lines stuffing their faces with limp beef burger and imitation chips.

As it happens they were pleased – I'd almost say relieved to see me, because they wanted to ask me a question. Believe it or not, they wanted to know the best way of getting pregnant. Jane, I mean, not Robert, obviously, and also the whole bit about what to expect during pregnancy, childbirth and beyond. I know, you would have thought at their age they would know about the birds and the bees, or endangered species in the world those two inhabit, which, come to think about it, was maybe why they wanted to know about sex, since all the animals they studied also seemed to have either never learned, or forgotten how to do it – hence them being endangered in the bloody first place.

It seems every time Jane had tried to ask her mother, you know, Clueless Cleo, all the woman would say is that it was perfectly natural, and they should go spend a day in the country observing how horses and cows do it, on the basis that Jane and Robert were committed environmentalists.

All that seems to have done is give Robert a fetish for asking Jane if she will give him piggy backs and since that didn't seem to be doing the trick at all, it left Robert in a state of frustration and Jane with lumbago.

As for giving birth and bringing up children, Jane's mother apparently said it was 'all just common sense', which proves to me that the stupid women is as deluded as ever and has clearly forgotten that if it hadn't been for the help she received from her own mother, instead of Jane ending up as a more or less normal young women, mooning to police officers from zip wires excluded, the girl would probably have ended up selling vacuum cleaners to satisfy her mother's fetish for the bloody things.

But before I tell you about my talk with the newlyweds, let me say that you have my sympathy for the way the council treated you after your argument with the bin men – or refuse technicians as we are now obliged to call them.

Anyone could have made your mistake in putting those incontinence pads in the wrong bin – with six to choose from, each with their own odour code, it was an easy error to make. If it wasn't bad enough that health service cuts were making you use the pads twice anyway.

If you ask me, it was adding insult to injury and nappy rash that the 'environmental crime team' made you attend that re-education class on waste reduction instead of a £150 fine (which, as you know, is more than you get for nicking a car). Looking on the bright side, at least the 'waste management' course didn't have anything to do with liposuction, from which I am certain Maude would benefit.

Anyway, back to my talk with the confused newlyweds. As you know, Reg, I am somewhat of an expert in all aspects of parenting and am the proud father of two grown up children who take the trouble to visit Maude and me at least once every 12 months (though this is usually to borrow one of my woodwork tools, which I never see again).

Still, I was surprised to be consulted on matters of procreation when I met the both of them in the village wholefoods shop – you know, the one with joss sticks that stink the place out and the shop assistant who wears beads through her nose and drones on about the cosmic energy of Stonehenge.

As far as I'm conerened, the only cosmic energy that one's ever experienced is that time when she sat on a carelessly discarded laser pen and as the shaft of light shone between her legs screamed out that she had undergone an Immaculate Conception from some ancient Druid or other. She still walks with a bit of a limp, well more of a hop, really. Some of those laser pens are very powerful you know.

You may well ask what I was doing at a whole-foods shop in the first place given the well-balanced diet I enjoy of chips and onion gravy twice daily, excepting when Maude has fallen out with me and I'm on chicken-ding, courtesy of the microwave.

Well, I was there at Maude's royal command to request they stop selling salted peanuts to my toothless mother-in-law since. As you know, they are lethal when she sucks the salt off them and then spits them out, taking aim at anything she dislikes – which usually means me. As I remonstrated with the women with beads through her nose, the happy couple were stocking up on tofu, seeds and something called 'unpolished whole grains'.

From what I could see of them, they were both underweight and looked as though they needed my special diet of toffee, seed buns stuffed with beef burger and polished off with as much profiterole & ice cream as their digestive systems, or bank balance, allowed.

When they asked me the question about sex, I made the point that they would need to feed themselves up if they had any hope of having children, on the basis that they may as well get some decent food while they could still afford it.

Jane told me that they had lived together in some sort of anti-global warming commune, which presumably meant they cooked food over a hot magnifying glass and stored ice-cubes ready to shore up the polar ice caps when they melt from the north ... and south, if you know what I mean, and presumably converge on Clapham Common.

She said that even though they had been together for several years, they had been 'saving themselves' for each other – a bit like not having your cake or eating it. It may be presented as the healthy option but in my book it also makes you a miserable sod – perhaps I should mention the subject to Maude now we are reaching the age of sexual dementia.

Undaunted by the challenge, I took them next door and sat them down for a cup of coffee that took ten minutes to order because the little shit who insisted he was a 'Barista' not 'the coffee bloke' as I had called him, took me through sixty-eight different fecking drink options in four sizes – none of them in English. I told him all I wanted was three cups of milky coffee and three sticky buns.

What I actually got was three tall glasses with enough whipped cream on top to keep a swingers' party happy; three tiny biscuits wrapped in posh plastic and marked 'fresh from our boutique bakery' and a penny change from ten quid.

By the time I scooped the cream out of the glass and tossed it over my shoulder with the deftest of flicks using the longest spoon you've ever seen in your life, the two mouthfuls of coffee the glass actually contained was cold.

As I started to explain things to my two eager young students of all things carnal, there was commotion behind us.

It seems that a somewhat fleshy women had slipped on the whipped cream carpet I had inadvertently laid down before her, and we were asked to leave on account I was, according to 'Barista Boy', a 'Waft Tat'.

Asking him what he was talking about, he replied by querying if I was any good at anagrams. I still haven't a clue what the stupid boy was talking about.

Elsewhere in the establishment, I could hear coffee cups, of which the place had obviously bought a job lot from the set of the latest Gulliver's Travels movie, smashing as men with arthritic right hands caused by their misspent youth and too much time on their hands, so to speak, failed to hold the weight of their not so piccola sized cups.

This caused them to break into a thousand pieces as they hit the already shrapnel damaged ceramic floor tiles. No wonder the coffee is so bloody expensive if they're having to buy new cups all the time.

After taking my revenge on Barista Boy by not leaving him a tip and telling him I had much better use for the penny change that in normal circumstances I'd have told him to keep, I found a quiet bench overlooking the village green to sit on and spent an unpleasant few minutes shovelling the bird crap off the seat.

It was at such times that I regretted spending so much effort throwing anything to hand at the cat owned by the fool over the fence that is my neighbour, since for once, it could have done something more useful than crapping amongst my dahlias and, instead, blunted its teeth on the pigeons that had obviously took a liking to this particular bench.

I did, however, start my talk by telling the two of them that the boy from Barista, or wherever he came from, was as good a reason as any NOT to have children.

Giving my young students the benefit of my vast experience, I set the scene by exploding some myths about getting pregnant. For instance, that:

a)   Just kissing, even with tongues, isn't enough to conceive, and that they should not confuse this with 'talking in tongues', which involved murmuring gibberish, holding both hands aloft then collapsing as if hit by a shaft of light. In reality any such collapse is likely to have been more to do with opening their electricity bill than anything from a heavenly body.

b)   Drinking powdered wolf's penis would not only result in failure but be likely to piss the wolf off no end, since it wouldn't have an end anymore. Not only that, but the powdered form can, I am told, bring on a sort of howling cough due to its dusty nature and in any case, the majority, whether in solid or powdered form, is highly likely to be fake on account that wolves can run faster than blokes with knives trying to castrate them and there are only twelve remaining in the world, mostly in Yellowstone Park in the US.

c)   So, any fool buying this supposed remedy is, in all likelihood, chomping on a freeze-dried sausage made to look like a wolf's wolf-hood through the cunning addition of the trapper's fingertip in an attempt to fool the purchaser that he had injured himself on their behalf as he went about his dangerous business. I also cautioned against buying the cheaper alternative of fox penis, since this would be much smaller in stature, likely to lead to the purchaser developing a tendency to rummage through neighbourhood refuse bins, and that the source could not be vouched for unless you happened to see the local male population of foxes looking depressed and walking with a peculiar gait.

d)   The old chestnut that standing on one's head afterwards will do the trick. This is most unlikely to work, especially if it's the man who does the headstands. My theory on this subject is that the male sperm is genetically programmed to swim upstream, so to speak, or at the very least, horizontally. If the lady stands upside down, this will only serve to confuse the sperm, especially if there is a preponderance of male sperm, since men are easily confused, have little sense of direction, get tired very quickly and would rather watch telly than undertake physical exercise of any sort. Also, doing headstands after sex can be dangerous since, if it is not done immediately, there is a danger that work colleagues in the office will not understand why their colleague is propped up against the wall with her legs in the air at a jaunty angle and devoid of underwear, while leading a video conference with a client about the merits of natural hair paint brushes, which, from the client's perspective, will look as though the model she is demonstrating has no visible handle.

e)   I especially made the point that having sex very frequently does not work since it just made the man walk with a gait that meant he couldn't stop a pig in an alleyway, and in any case, too much sex made you tired and caused headaches. It seemed to me to be an irony that when the man said he had a headache, the woman didn't believe him and he would often have to make his own tea, but that when a woman said she had a headache, the man was accused of being an insensitive pig with a sex addiction, and would be made to make his own tea. I have found that, over the years, this state of affairs has certain advantages in that I am now completely self-sufficient at making my own tea.

f) That heating her new husband's nuts will encourage sperm to be active. Saying that I was aware of the medical research that found a correlation between crotch temperature and male fertility, I cautioned against applying direct heat to the affected areas since this would likely result in Robert beating the Olympic high jump record, resent having singed pubic hair and in any case, the noxious smells from most proprietary topical creams or sprays (which, in any event are not designed for such purposes) would not be conducive to lovemaking on account that it would induce gagging and watery eyes, which though, in normal circumstances, might be an indicator of a good session, would, in this context, lead to much dissatisfaction, though remarkably clear nostrils.

g)   Similarly, Robert wearing loose underwear, though, I understand, scientifically proven to increase the number of sperm, may, on the surface, have certain advantages; ease of access, for instance. However, the downside is that Robert will feel as though his testicles are swinging in the wind and, if caught napping when he sits down, will feel as though the council bin wagon has got him caught in its recycling machinery, which is not to be advised.

h)   That making hubby his favourite meal will put him in the mood. I commented that while bribery has its place, and lavishing Robert with love and attention is a laudable pursuit, over-feeding him may backfire since he is more likely to fall asleep instead of fulfilling his marital duties, unless, of course, she is able to continue without his consciousness being necessarily required, in which circumstances it would be a case of 'win-win' as our American cousins are fond of saying; Robert gets fed and has a kip; Jane gets pregnant and since Robert will be in no position to move, Jane will not have to resort to standing on her head to no useful end, so to speak.

In order to put the young couple at their ease, for they were hanging on to my every word, which I thought much to their credit, I told them about my own honeymoon and that Maude had taken charge, saying she knew what to do.

Unfortunately, in those days it was sometimes the case that the mother-in-law came as well. And so, Maude's mother installed herself in the adjoining room in Mrs Baxter's 'Willow View' guest house on the promenade at Blackport.

Three meals a day (sometimes hot), one change of towels per couple and hot water on alternate days for 30 shillings a week each. I never did work out where the name came from given all you could see out of our window was the sewage outflow pipe making the sea turn an odd colour.

It was a bugger on rainy days since the old woman threw you out after each meal, dinner excepted when you could use the 'nicely appointed' TV lounge until 10.00pm, after which she turned the electricity off so you needed to be sharpish in getting into bed.

Anyway, on our wedding night, Maude told me to strip. I refused to take my socks off on account that Blackport in early March could still be a bit nippy and Maude said for me to turn lights out while she came out of bathroom 'with a surprise I would like'.

As my eyes adjusted to the darkness and the neon lights shining through the plastic curtains advertising the local whelk stall, I could just make out that she was wearing a waterproof raincoat, the hem of which she had taken up since she said that now we were married I was allowed to see her knee caps.

Apparently, her mother had told her that 'wearing rubber prevented pregnancy' and this had stood the woman well during World War II. Stupid woman – naive as I was, even I knew the difference between *wearing a rubber* and slinging a rubber *rain coat* over your bloody shoulders and telling me not to undo the buttons 'in case it leaked and got her pregnant'.

Well, anyway, Maude jumped on me as I lay expectantly on top of the bed but slid straight off me on account of the olive oil she had smeared over her coat because, she explained, the bottle said it was 'extra virgin' and she thought it was for newlyweds to 'help things run smoother'.

The stupid woman poleaxed herself on the headboard and let out such a scream that the mother-in-law rushed in and accused me of being a sex maniac and that I should have contented myself with, as she put it, 'the Masonic position' – and here's me thinking all Masons did was role a trouser leg up and give each other a funny handshake.

Now I didn't know what they shook with their hands, but I was pretty sure it wasn't anything to do with rubber – but then again...

As Maude recovered her senses, relatively speaking, she muttered something about 'not realising it would be so slippery'. The mother-in-law gave me an indignant look and said:

"What's so hard – you're a man, aren't you?"

"I can assure you it isn't hard at all." I said. "She jumped, she landed, she overshot – what was I supposed to do?"

"That's the point, you stupid man," she replied. "If you'd have been hard, she would have had something to latch onto and wouldn't have hit the bloody wall."

"No," I said, "but at the speed she was travelling, I would have hit the ceiling – and anyway, what's all that rubbish you've been telling her about wearing a rubber rain coat?"

"Rubber rain coat – what are you talking about?" she said.

I could then see that the terrible truth dawned on the old woman as she gave Maude a protective look before saying:

"Come with me while I rub something on your head and leave your nasty new husband to his own dirty doings."

"Safer than olive oil and flying rubber," I said.

"I don't know what she sees in you, I told her you were useless."

"And I told Maude she'd better not turn out like you or I'd go to sea."

With that, both of them turned to leave the room and gave me a perfectly synchronised death stare. I have to tell you, Reg, that I still can't abide the smell of rubber.

More than that, every time I see Maude putting her raincoat on I feel a funny do coming on and it makes me want to head for the shed and my woodwork tools.

Sparing my impressionable young students the gruesome detail of Maude and her mother, I told them it was best to be in the same room when doing it because it was quicker and you could go straight to sleep afterwards.

I told them that the alternatives were more expensive and who the hell wanted sextuplets just because the lab technician couldn't count?

By way of explaining what could go wrong if they didn't rely on more traditional methods of conception, I explained that I hadn't trusted the profession since being sent to the medical centre to give a sputum sample for a suspected chest infection, caused by inhaling too much hardwood dust making security gates to keep mother-in-law out of my shed (she keeps trying to pinch my long-nosed pliers to trim her nose hair).

When I got to the clinic they gave me a little plastic bottle, showed me into a room and told me to take at least 30 minutes because 'the quality would be higher'. I have to tell you, Reg, after 5 minutes I was bored, so put the TV on, which I thought strange for a room the size of a bus shelter – only to find every channel had a porn movie playing.

Then I noticed a pile of men's magazines and after my 30 minutes were up I handed over my sputum sample in the little plastic bottle. The nasty buggers threw me out for being a pervert and wasting their time.

I told the newlyweds that, in my long experience of having children, the best strategy is to watch the TV news channel since this will make them bored, then switch to the sports channel since this will make them tired, before retiring to bed and think what children will bring them.

This will either give them a headache and the need to reach for any tablet whose name ends in 'pan' or will motivate them to procreate. I also reminded them to make sure that they removed all underwear before having sex, or friction burns would result, which hurt like hell. In addition, non-removal of underwear would cause the wife's legs to shoot up and down like a marionette, which is, in my opinion and personal experience, most unladylike and is likely to bring on an attack of vertigo.

Jane plucked up courage to ask me about sexual positions for lovemaking and said she had heard of a famous Indian book that had pictures of all the different ways it was possible to make love. I told her that she was correct. It was called the *Karma Sutra*. However, I warned her against getting carried away since many of the positions required the flexibility of a contortionist with masochistic tendencies, the imagination of a City football fan thinking they could win the cup and the stamina of a Himalayan marathon runner being chased by a Yeti.

I added that if Indian culture was something that inspired them, I recommended studying a menu from their local takeaway and think about what they could do with some onion bhajis, half a dozen poppadoms and a double portion of Bombay potatoes. While they would be too stuffed to make love, at least they would sleep well, safe in the knowledge that their bowels would be fully opened before the cock crowed, so to speak.

Sensing their disappointment, I suggested that if Indian food didn't appeal and they were intent on bankrupting themselves having children, then spending the rest of their lives trying to gain their affection before finally realising that the late show of interest from their children had more to do with getting your signature on a Power of Attorney (property *and* social), and their increasingly close attention to sold property prices in your road, then I recommended the missionary position.

I made this recommendation on the basis that if it was good for missionaries, then that was good enough for them. After all, Missionaries down the ages had converted a goodly proportion of the human race though the laying on of hands and their oral skills, so their system-based approach to sex must have been successful.

Either that or there had been a big mix up when they repeated the mantra 'there's many a slip between cup and lip'. Perhaps that's why they preferred the withdrawal method.

Robert said that he had also heard about the withdrawal method and did I think it any good. I responded by asking him to think about a time when he had a juicy sweet in his mouth and had he ever tried to keep it there without biting or chewing on it.

When he said it just wasn't possible I said that he had answered his own question and that the only way to make the withdrawal method work was to give himself the shock of his life at the crucial moment. Robert asked me what sort of shock might work.

I told him that when he felt the urge to complete his task, if you follow my meaning, he should either ask his wife to fully utilise the pelvic floor exercise she should have been practicing, or else call to mind his bank balance and how much he thought might remain in 12 months' time, what with the price of sleeping pills and all.

I said that each approach had their advantages, but that the former would result in a non-surgical vasectomy, the latter would result in a permanent state of depression.

Asking him to consider these options carefully after some minutes he said that thinking about it, some men he worked with had said you could usually return to work the next day after a vasectomy. I didn't have the heart to tell him the truth and nodded at him in a sage like way.

I finished off telling them about the virtues of the missionary position by saying that it also had the advantage of causing the least confusion for inexperienced lovers, since they would be facing one another, but that if they could only see each other's toes, one of them would be at the wrong end of the bed.

I emphasised that this was something which should be corrected immediately to avoid any risk of an STI (sucked toe incident), since this might necessitate an expensive visit to a chiropodist, or at the very least, the need to lay in an ample supply of corn plasters.

My young students seemed satisfied enough with my explanation, but I sensed that they wanted to discuss positioning in more detail. You could say that my decades of experience from being married to Maude made me an expert of such things. Yes, you could say that, I wouldn't, since it isn't true.

It wouldn't be true because the Queen only has two birthdays a year, Maude prepares meticulously for such occasions, and I take copious amounts of whisky so that I can't remember. The only reminder that the twice-yearly events have passed is an overriding urge to melt Maude's rubber rain coat, plus a slight limp in both legs that generally eases if I massage my men's bits with fish oil. It doesn't do anything for the pain, but it puts Maude off long enough for her carnal thoughts to subside until the Queen has another birthday.

How am I qualified to give the newlyweds the benefit of my wisdom then, I hear you say. Well, that bit of voluntary work I do taking library books to the old folk's home in the village means that I often find myself inadvertently walking into the bedroom of residents 'at it', sometimes on their own, at other times in pairs (all combinations) and on rare occasions, on a group basis.

It seems the staff turn a blind eye on the basis that such activities are most unlikely to lead to a pregnancy, and that if it does, it would be excellent publicity for the home. My only concern is that on more than one occasion a member of staff has pointed me to the appropriate room assuming I am a resident or visiting pensioner at an away game.

The positions they get themselves into defy age and brittle bone disease and have taught me many things that I am determined to keep from Maude, though I do know that the mother-in-law visits the home occasionally and always returns with flushed cheeks, her hair piece at a jaunty angle and false teeth cement all around her chops.

So, I ran the young couple through a variety of positions that seemed to alarm them more with each new idea I introduced. Jane just couldn't get the wheelbarrow position on account, she said, that she wouldn't have a wheel to push along.

Robert commented that he didn't fancy doing it standing up since he was a lot taller than Jane and he was worried things might not fit properly.

Alas they both got upset when I started talking about tantric sex, on account that a couple they were friendly with at the protest camp had a dog called tantric and that they weren't into that sort of thing at all, even if some animals were in danger of extinction since there was only so far their environmental beliefs would take them.

I gave up and told them to stick to the missionary position, but to remember what I said about not sucking each other's toes unless they had decided not to have any children, or they had hard skin from wearing all those organic non-genetically-modified straw sandals.

To lighten the mood, I ended this bit of my talk by telling them that they would know when their efforts in taking off all their underwear had been successful because their feelings for one other would begin to change, insofar as Jane would start to throw up over him every morning and he would start to get death stares for making her ill.

***

Next, I explained the process they would go through as the pregnancy progressed. I told them it was perfectly natural that they begin to obsess about the little display on those pregnancy testing pen-thingies, and that two distinct phases would follow:

(a)   They will both laugh

(b)   They would start to cry, then cry a lot more

I emphasised that this would be quite normal as they realised that nothing at all would be normal again. You'll remember, Reg, that we didn't have such things in our day.

The first inkling I got that something peculiar was occurring was that Maude started eating lumps of coal for no apparent reason, which, given the price of the stuff, caused several arguments.

In this I felt totally justified since I resented waking up every morning to coal dust hanging in the air and the sight of Maude with a ring of tar around her gob, which was even worse than the curlers and headscarf she wore in bed anyway.

I always appreciated the friendly ear you gave me when I sounded off about not having enough coal to light a fire. For my part, I always felt sorry for you when your better half fell pregnant.

At this junction I told the newlyweds that in 'falling pregnant' it was a myth that 'falling' caused pregnancy – unless it involves falling on the tool specifically designed for the job, so to speak.

Thinking about it, I suppose that these days such tools might also include a Petri dish, pipette or, the way things are going, an iPhone App. Now it's not that I'm against technology. In fact, I recognise that technology has many advantages, including no need to forgo your favourite news programme on telly in favour of the ubiquitous 'early night'.

Then again, missing the first 10 minutes or so isn't too big a sacrifice, is it? Plus, you can always watch on 'catch-up TV' these days. Anyway, back to your good lady's pregnancy, I knew you were having it hard in coping with June's fetish for pickled eggs with crème-fresh because of that unfortunate incident when police accused you of gross indecency.

I've always believed you, Reg, when you said your drink was spiked, and that when the police found you collapsed in that alleyway with a white liquid substance round your mouth and what appeared to be your testicles on display, you were innocent and on an urgent errand for your wife.

It didn't help that the female police officer fainted as her colleague helped you up and the empty little tubs of crème-fresh made it look like your nuts were rolling down the drain.

Getting back to the newlyweds, I next explained the joy of announcing to the world that you are going to have a little baby (ever thought why everyone always says 'little' baby, Reg? What other sort are there until they start to eat you out of house and home?). In my own case all the mother-in-law said was.

"What took you so long and don't be expecting me to do all the baby-sitting. I suppose you will be wanting nappies then? They cost a fortune, you know."

At the mention of nappies, I explained to the young couple that they had a decision to make. Did they follow the modern trend and opt for the disposable kind – though if you happened to be a bin man in the height of summer, I don't suppose you would think that they were disposable for one minute – or if they were, he wished you would dispose of them in a bin he didn't have to empty.

Of course, the use of the word 'disposable' was a misnomer, on the basis that they have a half-life of 20 years and stink the back yard out, courtesy of council's environmental policy of collecting bins every 2nd partial eclipse of the sun and fostering the expansion of the bluebottle fly population. I tell you, having to wear a gas mask to hang out the washing isn't funny when you hate the smell of rubber in the first place.

I then explained that a second choice would be to use traditional towelling nappies. Yes, expensive, but useable time and time again by first sluicing the contents of your little prince or princess's increasingly vengeful bowels down the toilet (or sink, if the missus is out), then boiling them until the whole house smells of Brussels sprouts, the flies go on holiday and even double- glazing salesmen give your house a miss.

Thinking about it, Reg, perhaps we're missing a trick here in not inventing an air not-freshener that you can hang above the front door that stinks of baby poo. We could call it 'Stink-u-away'.

Almost in unison, the newlyweds said that because of their commitment to the environment, they would want to use traditional nappies.

When I said that their neighbours wouldn't thank them for stinking *their* environment to high heaven, Jane said that losing the friendship of the neighbours would be a small price to pay for saving the world from gaseous emissions. I said that on that basis, they had better buy a doll since the real thing pumped enough foul crap out on a daily basis to power Battersea power station.

I told them that they would have to factor in the cost of baby clothes since these could be expensive and that babies don't stay little for very long. I recounted that when my children were born, we received unsolicited and unwanted gifts of 'pre-owned' baby clothes from all and sundry that looked as if they were rejects from the rag and bone man.

Either that or they had been hand knitted by some demented aunt and which made babies look like tea cosies – or those little plastic dolls with knitted dresses that covered the spare toilet roll.

So, I warned them to beware of such 'friends' that were, in reality, just trying to offload a loft full of tat to the next sucker who had be as naïve as them when they had their first child.

Jane corrected me by saying that the trend 'these days' was to have a 'baby shower party'. I said it sounded like it was some sort of secret communal bathing ritual for women, where they swapped stories of waters breaking and compared stretch marks. Jane said that wasn't the case at all and that the event went on all day and even included men.

It was all I could do to shake my head and say I found the idea most strange and asked her again if these parties had anything to do with water. She said they didn't and it was an idea that had come over from America.

I said that it now all made sense and we had imported yet another idea from the land that gave us television adverts, powdered egg and beef burgers that never rot.

As I warmed to my theme of the progression of the pregnancy, I explained about the mysterious world of the anti-natal clinic, when Robert would lose all sense of his own identity or personality, instead simply being referred to as 'dad' by staff.

I warned him that this strange form of address would lead to excessive bouts of him turning his head from side to side and compulsive turning around wondering who the hell they were talking about. He would be required to watch birth videos that would put him off his dinner;

demonstrations using a rubber doll and a simulated birth canal that would put him off his wife.

Then there would be the woeful tales from attendees who had given birth before that would make him want to end his life. I added that if he successfully survived this rite of passage, when it came to them having their second and subsequent children, he would be in a position, and would enjoy, terrorising all the new fathers he would come across with apocryphal tales of blood, guts and camera phones – with sound.

And then there were the exercises that Robert would be required to encourage and motivate Jane to complete on a regular basis in preparation for the happy event. Foremost amongst these would be breathing exercises. Robert said that Jane knew perfectly well how to breathe, and any fool knew that it was just a case of sucking in and blowing out on a regular basis.

He over-acted the scenario by way of demonstrating his expertise at this skill. The boy became very confused when I explained the process to be applied during the birth and I demonstrated the technique of rapid breathing and its purpose in providing the maximum amount of oxygen to the baby at a most critical time.

Ever seeking to please, Robert mimicked my demonstration with gusto. Rather too much gusto as it turned out since he hyperventilated, slid from the park bench and landed in a heap in a fresh pile of pigeon crap that tested their environmental credentials to the limit judging by his face when he regained consciousness.

Jane asked if she should prepare anything to have with her when she gave birth. I replied that this was a very good question and it absolutely was a case of 'be prepared'. I offered them the following by way of example:

Jane: change of nightie.

Robert: iPhone, iPod, iPad, ear plugs, sweets, crisps, money for fast food.

I cautioned them both that, as the birth neared, Jane would become more uncomfortable, would pass wind a lot and would need to be in rolling distance of a toilet at all times.

I stressed that a key responsibility of Robert would be to ensure that he was always on hand to pull Jane up from the chair, bed and any other surface that was not vertical, and that he should prepare by exercising his biceps, triceps and finger tips.

And also buying a sufficient quantity of muscular pain relief from the repetitive strain injury that was certain to result.

I emphasised that on no account should Robert make any derogatory remarks about Jane's increased use of her bottom to pass noxious odours, on account that it wasn't British to do, and in any case, it risked a sharp crack across the back of his head from his wife's angry fist.

I also cautioned that it would be at this point in the pregnancy that Jane would accuse Robert of all manner of imagined indiscretions, from looking at other women (not pregnant), to him innocently complaining about the food she cooked for him tasting of baby bottle sanitising fluid, to the fact that he didn't love her anymore because he wouldn't make love to her – despite the fact that to do so could well incur the wrath of the, until then, unborn child who would be quite entitled to complain about being born with a black eye, and that Robert would need crampons to hang on during proceedings.

***

Next, Jane asked my advice about the various forms of birth that were available and which I thought the most beneficial. This is a subjective question because it depends whose perspective is involved.

From a chap's point of view, hospital is always the first and best option since if anything goes wrong, like he has a panic attack or hurts his head when he faints, there will be ample well trained medical personnel on hand to tend his needs.

Many women, on the other hand, have romantic notions about giving birth at home. Now, while home births offer certain advantages; the easy availability of familiar foods and ready access to the TV remote, for example, there are risks inherent in not being amongst the odd thousand or two medical professionals within spitting, or should I say, grabbing distance from the expectant parents.

Home births can also give rise to complaints from neighbours about excessive noise disturbing their daytime television watching habits, or, if a night birth occurs, forced abandonment of their pay per view adult movies leading to heated arguments and requests for financial compensation on account of them having paid £3.99 to watch something likely called She-devil Nymphomaniacs, Werewolves go Dogging or Zombie Ride in the Park.

I also said that there was a third option, which was to 'go private'. The great advantage of giving the public sector the elbow and paying real cash money – or at least real plastic, was that it was possible to pre-select on which day and at what time you wished to join the serried ranks of depressed parenthood. In this way you would be teaching your child that from day one it had to work to your timetable.

Of course, Reg, I didn't have the heart to tell them that if they believed that, they were in for a life of bitter disappointment and much angst. Instead, I concentrated on the positives and continued to extol the virtues of private healthcare, including the luxury of walking on carpets your feet don't stick to, cups of tea made with real teabags and served in cups that would actually break if you dropped them, a choice of food that was made from ingredients known to man and, most importantly of all, a plentiful supply of 'his and hers' gas and air dispensers to render any memory of childbirth distant and ethereal.

In any event, I emphasised the need to make a decision and stick to it, since failure to do so would probably result in Robert delivering the baby himself on double yellow lines in town and being booked by the traffic police for failure to keep his hands on the steering wheel and endangering the public's safety by breeching the local noise abatement regulations.

Jane asked me who was with Maude and me in the 'delivery suite' when our eldest lad was due. I have to say, Reg, the question baffled me. By 'delivery suite' I assumed she meant the little cubical you couldn't swing a new born baby around in to fill its lungs with air, and badly photocopied signs all over the walls saying that abusive language or physical violence would not be tolerated, unless the perpetrator was the expectant mother and the focus of her efforts was the pig ignorant and sexual predator that passed for her husband.

I had my suspicions that the signs had been put up by some 'liberated' midwife with a chip on her shoulder, or more likely, a collection of men's shrunken heads, each suspended from her epaulettes on its owner's withered genitalia.

As for who else was in the room at the time, well, I got stumped after I listed Maude, me, the baby (eventually) and the occasional midwife who kept dropping hints about how easy is was to deliver a child, that any man could do it and anyway, she had to be away by 8.00pm to collect her elderly grandmother from the local Zumba class.

When I commented that the elderly lady deserved credit for keeping active, the midwife shrugged her shoulders and said the old women had been thrown out of every dance class within 10 miles of where they lived for sexually assaulting the male students. The plan was that Zumba classes would tire her out.

When I asked if it was working she said that she didn't think so, but at least her Gran had met a nice old gentleman and they spent their time in the back room playing doctors and nurses.

Seeing my surprised expression, the midwife explained that no sexual activities were involved, or at least she didn't think so. Instead they examined each other's pill box stamped with the days of the week, then played 'swapsies'.

She said that by the time she went to collect her Gran, the old woman would be fast asleep from having taken one of the old gentleman's sedatives, while he was usually to be found moaning in the toilets having overdosed on her Gran's diuretic tablets.

In response to me asking Jane who she thought should be at the birth, she mentioned something called 'birthing partners'.

Well, as you can imagine, I couldn't help pulling one of my rare confused faces because if you ask me, it sounds more like something you might do if the conception bit had involved one of those swinging parties you hear about that seems to go on so much in houses with two cars, one of which will be a, what do you call them, plus-fours – no, they're golfing pants aren't they – I mean four by fours; will live in a detached house south of the M25 and in all likelihood will have a timeshare flat in Marbella that they will describe as an exclusive Spanish custom-built villa to their friends – who, of course, never get to see the shoe box in the sun. Why swingers' parties? I hear you ask, Reg.

Well, if you don't know who was responsible for putting it in, you may as well hedge your bets and have them all present when it comes out, so you can compare hair colour. I suppose that could get a bit tricky if the baby is born without any hair and a couple of the swingers are also bald – the men, I mean, obviously.

While I'm on the subject of swingers' parties, of which I have no practical experience, Maude has mentioned them once or twice over the years and I have to say I have been very tempted on the basis that it feels selfish of me to deprive other men of Maude's presence in a rubber raincoat greased with vegetable oil. I stopped her using the extra virgin sort on the basis that it would be against the trades description act now.

The trouble that the woman, in her self-deluded mission to 'keep up with the young ones', now uses GM free sunflower oil. The only problem is she gets it cheap from the local fish and chip shop and it stinks to high heaven and has bits of potato and the crispy bits off the fish batter mixed in with it. And you wonder why I spend so much time in my shed, Reg.

So, I posed the inquisitive newlyweds a question. I asked if they intended to invite their parents, best friends, their cousins and the taxi driver that would bring them to the hospital, into the bedroom to witness their night of carnal pleasure when they hoped conception would happen – or, perhaps, they would offer a season ticket to the bedroom terraces to hedge their bets.

As expected, they gave me the sort of look that told me they wouldn't be eating for the next two days – not that I hadn't already mentioned that they look malnourished, what with all those lentils and seeds they swallow, so I didn't think they could afford to lose any more weight.

When Jane said she thought that was a horrible idea for something so intimate, I asked her why the hell she would want half of the village present at the birth of her child – and if she thought she moment of conception was intimate, how would she feel with every piece of electronic film gadget known to humanity being pointed at her thighs as she lay there with her legs akimbo, cousin Jeremy fainting over the midwife and spinster Aunty Gillian puking into the gas and air mask that she will have nicked from you as she cursed all men saying they – or at least their dangly bits – should burn in hell.

Jane thought for a moment in the way that those environmental sorts tend to do. You know, chin in hand, looking very earnest and nodding their head as if it came free with a car insurance policy.

"I hear what you say, but the birth-plan we'll put together will account for that contingency and we might, for example, ask them all to leave the room for the critical moment."

'Birth Plan', 'contingency', 'critical moment'. I couldn't believe what I was hearing, Reg. If the poor girl thought she would have any say when it came to it, she was even more deluded than I thought she was after she chained herself to that vacuum cleaner store after she heard a rumour that their latest model caused cyclones.

I blame her parents for the fetish they still have for 'hoovers' as we used to call them. Yes, I know, you're going to remind me I started it by sending that stripogram round to their house to demonstrate her suction hose in revenge for what Trevor did to me on my stag night, but I ask you, how could Jane confuse a TV ad for a cleaner with 'cyclone technology' for something that was about to flatten the village?

Anyway, as you might remember, the time she spent in gaol for assaulting that policeman with his own truncheon, which, by the way, I thought excessive, since it apparently never left his trousers, though I understand he still walks a little awkwardly, gave her ample time to push vacuum cleaners up and down the prison canteen and test out her theories on its ability to wreak havoc across the neighbourhood.

I detected that she had set her sights of formulating a birth plan, and sticking to it, though I thought she had gone too far when she started to explain the 'types' of birth it was possible to have these days.

"We intend to use a birthing pool," said Jane, with Robert nodding in passive agreement as they sat there holding hands, letting go of each other only to pick bits of stale pigeon crap from their shoulders that kept falling from the low hanging branches above them, and which had clearly been the roosting spot for a clutch of pigeons who had been for a boys night out on curry and lager the night before.

"We have considered the big rubber ball and birthing chair but thought these would be too traumatic for our child."

By now I was losing the will to live, Reg. I can understand why they decided to reject the rubber ball since it would be like giving birth on a trampoline, especially if the room is full of 'birthing partners' who are pinging themselves all over the room having fainted onto that stupid ball.

I can even understand why Jane rejected the 'birthing chair' since this is only a fancy modern name for a commode, but 'birthing pool'.

Yee Gods, does the girl not know that babies aren't born with water wings or a wet suite (if you ask me the only person that will be wearing a wet suite is Robert from getting too close to Jane when her waters break).

I know we've all seen pictures of that little baby apparently swimming by pushing its tongue out to stop water getting in. Seems to me that its parents just stuck a cork in to look like a tongue for the publicity and to earn a share of the advertising revenue on *YouTube*.

In order to bring some sanity back to our conversation, I suggested that the only other person who need be in the room, apart from essential medical staff, would be Robert – and then only to act as recipient of the sporadic bouts of verbal and physical abuse that Jane would want to lob in his direction.

I also suggested he abide by the following instructions in strict order of importance for his own wellbeing, safety and minimisation of bruising:

a)   Take up position at head of bed and do not move under any circumstances unless ordered out of the room by medical staff, or you catch sight of an open door and believe you have a good chance of escaping through it before Jane has the opportunity to manhandle him back into position.

b)   Keep an obsessive check on the little gauge above Jane's head because this will tell him how much gas and air is left. If it reads low, insist that the midwife replenishes the supply. If she fails to act and the supply fails, run from the room and stay out.

c)   Remember to place a small foam ball in palm of his hand, so that when Jane crushes his fingers during her contractions, they have something to nestle into instead of shattering bones in the palm of his hand and causing nail penetration wounds to his delicate skin.

d)   Keep in mind the saying that 'many a true word is said in jest,' but that it should really be 'many a true word is said in labour'. This is because Jane will really tell him what she thinks, including: 'twat' for getting her pregnant; 'lazy twat' for not doing anything to help during pregnancy and 'selfish twat' for not keeping her in sufficient supply of sardines and onion bhajis when she was in need.

e)   That 'phantom pains' for fathers do not exist. Nor are they to be given any credence for being psychosomatic due to him naturally wanting to empathise with his wife's pain. No, any pain he will feel will be physical, because he will have the bruises to prove it was all down to Jane punching him in the stomach in retribution for her then current state. I said that if he suffers a headache he will have only himself to blame as he bends too close to his wife's head, albeit understandably to bath her brow with some soothing balm or other. In reality she will simply head-butt him as she is told to 'push' by the midwife, then, as her contraction subsides, hit him again for making her forehead hurt.

f)   That babies come from behind green sheets. I gave him the benefit of my own experience in that when Maude was told to lay on the bed and stick her legs in those things that are also useful for repairing shoes, a big green sheet was placed on a sort of scaffolding that hid everything south of Maude's waist. I assume this was to keep the area sterile and, of course, protect my eyes from bodily fluids that were not mine (not strictly speaking, anyhow), and images of a gynaecological nature that might put me off my tea. I urged him to repeat this mantra, to subdue any inquisitive notions he might have if he had not fainted by then, and under no circumstances whatever to accept the invitation of a midwife waiting to do her party-piece by suggesting she could just see the child's hair, when, in fact, she pulls the child out just as the wary husband peeks over the green sheet and gets whiplashed by the umbilical cord. I warned Robert that if he was fool enough to get caught by the midwife entertaining herself at his expense, he should retreat or he would end up wearing the afterbirth as a necklace – and a knobbly one at that.

g)   If he was lucky enough to end up with a midwife with any sense of decency and appreciation of his feelings, she would ask him to leave the room as the baby's head is about to be born so that they can do whatever checks they need to do. I emphasised that on no account should he look back to look at his wife – or her bottom half anyway, since the sight is, in my opinion, where the Greek's got their notion of the Medusa from.

h)   When sent out of the room he should try not to be too inquisitive of events taking place in the adjoining cubicles, or 'delivery suites' which Jane continued to insist on calling them.

I told him of my own experience in foolishly taking out the earplugs I had taken care to purchase some weeks previously. Actually, that wasn't strictly what happened.

They had both been ejected when Maude head-butted me for the third time and I was too dizzy to find them as the midwife ordered me out of the room. Anyway, it meant that I had no choice but to listen to the women next door as I stood against the corridor wall as if I was waiting to enter the headmaster's study.

I said to Robert that for all Maude's failings, and there were many, most of them relating to her looks, observance of Her Majesty's two birthdays per year, and the high pitched modulation in her voice when she shouted at me that made my ears sore, the woman was as quiet as a church mouse when giving birth to our children – the odd grunt and several bouts of farting, yes, but I suppose that was understandable; I myself am a martyr to flatulence if I eat too many of Maude's chick-peas, so who am I to comment?

Anyway, as I waited outside Maude's room, the woman next door started making the strangest noises I'd ever heard. Everything from a 'whoop, whoop' to a type of growl, then onwards to a full-throated scream that would have shattered a crystal chandelier.

It was then that I understood where the sound effects man got his material for the filming of the *Hound of the Baskervilles*. And if that wasn't bad enough, a little later on, I saw two women in white wellies and aprons mopping the room out.

Eventually I was told to come back in and the midwife asked if I wanted to see the baby's head being born. I told Robert that I was far too busy concentrating on the gas and air gauge to be distracted by the sight of my child being born. It was only then that I noticed a trainee midwife had joined us in the room. It was more the fact that her face had drained of colour that caught my attention.

Now I had a dilemma; do I keep watch on the gas and air gauge, or do I ask if anything is wrong while all the time saying to myself that the big green sheet is still in place, so everything must be going to plan and that at any moment my new child will crawl up the sheet and give me a cheery wave.

Then I see the trainee midwife look at the real midwife, who is giving the trainee daggers for looking as if she is terrified, because the real midwife knows I am looking at the woman with the pale white face and that if she's terrified, I'm even more terrified. I told Robert that it was then I noticed the real midwife surreptitiously slipping the terrified one the biggest pair of spatulas I've ever seen, and a pair of what looked like decorators' scissors.

Keeping faith in the big green vertical sheet, I heard what sounded like a sink plunger sucking tealeaves from the u-bend, followed by a crisp 'snip' and it was job done. The colour returned to the training midwife's cheeks, while the real midwife headed next door to see to whaling Winnie.

Jane said that it must have been a wonderful moment and that it was something you would remember for the rest of your life. I said that yes, in one way, it was something you remembered, especially the part when the trainee midwife held my first-born upside down and held him aloft as if she was going to hang him from the ceiling to dry.

Do you know, Reg, that boy still suffers from vertigo and I would bet the mother-in-law's false teeth that his condition was cause by hanging upside down for so long.

You'd have thought they'd have invented some sort of baby drier by now – you know, the sort that you get in posh hotels where you slide your hand in and out of the thing without touching the sides. Well, perhaps they could design something similar for babies – you know, a sort of car wash without all those plastic roller things that tear your wing mirrors off.

Come to think of it, it would be too dangerous, and we would end up with a preponderance of pre-circumcised male babies, or even transgender – but then I suppose that could save the health service tons of money in the long run, couldn't it? Perhaps not, eh, Reg?

Anyway, the trainee midwife finished air-drying the lad then announced to Maude and me that we had 'a beautiful little boy'. I don't know about you, Reg, but I think most new-borns are ugly blighters with heads too big for their bodies, faces that look like an iceberg lettuce and, as far as boy babies go, a nasty habit of peeing in your chops whenever your face is within range.

Do you think they are born with some sort of primeval sensor that allows them to get first blood in before they spend the next 16 years being told what to do by their parents? Or are they just practicing for when they are eighteen and can't hold their beer – it's a strange world if you ask me.

I told the eager newlyweds that shortly after my son was born, something very strange happened. They both looked at me intently, as if I was about to reveal the meaning of life. Perhaps in a way, I was, because once the trainee midwife handed the baby over to Maude, who was still comatose in the bed, staring up at the ceiling as if in a trance, a peaceful hush descended on the place; the baby fell asleep and was quiet for the first and last time in his life, and I was left wondering what was for tea.

***

I may have told you before, Reg, but the last thing that occurred to me once I got home from the hospital to prepare to bring baby and Maude home the following day was my tea. Why? Because something strange had happened. Initially I thought we'd been burgled.

My woodwork books and the tools I had been sharpening on the dining table had disappeared. I sat down to watch a bit of TV and noticed the channel had been changed from the one I had left it on.

No longer was I listening to the dulcet tones of my favourite sports commentator, instead some woman was droning on about twenty uses for lemon you'd never heard before – and after she'd finished I never wanted to hear them again, let me tell you. But the biggest shock came went I went upstairs for a wee.

The toilet seat was inexplicitly in the closed position and where before there had been two spare toilet rolls, there now stood two dolls with hand knitted dresses covering said toilet rolls.

Worse than that, there was a hand-written note stuck to the cold tap with the words 'You have a baby now, so fix the drip'. I was perplexed, why would Maude leave me notes when I'd just left her in the hospital? The mystery continued when I went into the child's bedroom and discovered the cradle I had hand made in readiness for the happy event had been moved to our bedroom.

Now I was convinced we had been burgled – but why would a thief leave me a note about a dripping tap. Coming downstairs and into front room I saw that the sofa had been made up as a bed and some of my clothes were stacked neatly on one of the chairs.

Now the terrible truth hit me. No burglary had taken place, no thief had left me a note and no lightfingered lout had decided to take up residence in the front room. It was worse than that, much, much worse.

The mother-in-law was moving in for the duration. Just then my worst fears were realised when the front door opened. A familiar shrill voice pierced the air that led to a mass exodus of assorted insects knowing their time was up if they stayed. I swear I also heard our resident mouse nailing up the entrance to its little den.

"So, you're back then, I hope you've left our Maude and the lad in good order or there'll be no tea for you, new father or not."

"It's nice to see you," I lied before trying to find out how long she intended to stay.

"For a week and that's all there is to it. You can make do with the sofa in the front room because they'll be none of that hanky panky stuff for quite some time, our Maude has to get her strength back; she can't be bothered with men's doings. I've made your bed up on the sofa and put some clothes out.

All the rest I've chucked out because there're either falling apart or not fit to be around a new baby. And another thing, have you fixed that tap yet, we can't have that keeping our Maude awake, you know."

Although I was not yet old or experienced enough to stand up to my mother-in-law's domineering nature and one that Maude was rapidly acquiring, I reflected on two things: The pressure would be off me as far as the 'men's doings' were concerned, and it seemed to me that if I was banished to the front room, I could hardly be blamed if I failed to hear the child if it might cry out for attention.

In any event, with two women in the house, one only slightly less cuckoo than the other, I reasoned that my new son would get all the attention a helpless chap could wish for.

Anyway, I spent the rest of the evening keeping out of the mother-in-law's clutches by repairing the leaking tap and leaving the toilet seat up just to annoy her. I also found out where she had thrown my best work clothes, retrieved them and hid them in the shed, pending reinstatement once the woman had gone back to her coven.

And so, the day to bring baby home arrived and I knew that Maude had recovered from childbirth because she started to boss me about again, only this time her every command was tinged with that 'make sure you do it properly so no harm comes to baby' blackmail type voice.

Another thing I noticed was that I ceased to exist in my own right. Now my only purpose was to 'get this' for baby or 'do that' for baby. As the lad grew older nothing really changed except he spoke on his own behalf with every sentence beginning with 'I want'.

That was, except for the phase between twelve and fifteen, when he didn't speak at all and only came out of his bedroom for food and to use the toilet. And now? Well, the language has changed but the result is still the same insofar as he usually starts his sentences with 'would you mind if I borrowed...' which I know I will never see whatever he's borrowing again.

When I explained this process to the newlyweds they commented, almost in unison, that it would be different with their children and that things were more modern now.

I hadn't the heart to tell them children never change, and it seemed to me the only thing that had really changed was that their kids wouldn't need to speak to them at all.

They would just send a text, email or leave a message for them on Facebook asking them what was for tea, could they lend them some money or they were leaving home because their parents were uncaring sods who never even talked to them. Oh, the joys of parenthood!

I did warn Robert that irrespective of whether his mother-in-law installed herself for the baby's homecoming, there would be a number of things that he would notice. These would include:

a)   A surreal feeling of calm before the storm that he may have experienced for a short time in the delivery suite. Wife asleep, baby asleep, mother-in-law absent (at home this would be because she would be busy writing a list of things for Robert to do, fix or make).

b)   The mother-in-law will keep feeding you the same meal. This may be out of spite, lack of culinary skills or some warped gesture to please you since you may have made the mistake of complimenting her on some dish she made at some point in time.

In my case this was shepherd's pie. I made the simple, stupid mistake several years earlier when Maude first took me for tea at her mother's house by complimenting her on the dish, which in reality was crap and full of gristle – but I was still young and callow and too frightened not to eat what she put on the table.

God, how I paid for that cowardice.

c)   Strange, noxious smells will start to permeate the house, not unlike a mixture of damp cardboard and mushy peas. Some may say they are of course, one and the same thing. Eventually you will trace this danger to life as coming from the backside of your heir.

I stressed to Robert that it was at this point he had to be careful in not giving in to the demands of wife and mother-in-law to change baby's nappy.

It seems to me that there are certain jobs which men are just not cut out to do. It's bad enough that we're expected to unblock any drains that require attention, cook when it comes to BBQs despite not knowing one end of a lamb's leg from the other, and we're always expected to be the one to change the car tyre – even if not in the car at the time.

I am happy to report that I have never changed a nappy in my life, though my daughter-in-law's threat not to change my colostomy bag when that unhappy time comes if I don't agree to change my grandchild's nappy is beginning to play on my mind somewhat, though I'm maintaining a brave face when in her presence for the time being while I formulate a suitably believable plan to escape my fate.

  d)   One morning he will wake up happy, in fact he will feel very happy. At first, he will feel confused, then assume it is simply the powerful range of emotions that come with having a new baby. Then it will finally dawn; the mother-in-law has gone home. He has manned-up by refusing her kind offer to stay another week on the basis that she needs to cook some more shepherd's pie and at last, at last, he has the house to himself, apart, that is, from a wife who seems to cry without reason and a baby that clearly doesn't have to have a reason to cry.

  e)   To check any food that his wife cooks him carefully for the first few weeks. I explained that this is a time of great confusion for new mothers. They have many crisis of confidence as they worry if they will be a good enough mother. They will have a crises of self-image as they wonder if their husbands will still desire them and they will have a crisis of memory as they wonder where they left those safety pins they know they had before they started making their husband's meal.

  f) After a few weeks, if Jane is anything like Maude was, she will tentatively begin to ask the health visitor, and I put this delicately, when 'relations' might begin again and that he should make every effort to bribe the health visitor into telling his wife such things should be left for six months. I knew something was up when one day, Maude cooked me my favorite tea and told me about the conversation she had had with the health visitor. Luckily Maude said that the Queen's birthday wasn't for another few months. I felt this took the pressure off, gave me plenty of time to prepare, and also write to the Palace to enquire if the Queen wouldn't mind moving her birthday to a leap year; alas I didn't receive a response from Her Majesty.

By way of lifting the mood, I told my eager students that life would quickly settle into a routine that would involve Robert going to work, coming home, having tea (after checking the gravy for foreign objects).

I also found time to sharpen my chisels, patting the baby on its head and saying, 'sleep tight don't let the bed bugs bite'. He seemed to take delight in throwing up on me in reply. Then it was off to bed to prepare for a hard day's work the next day.

Jane asked me how I dealt with all those disturbed nights that you hear so much about. I explained that I had also heard such things, but that interrupted sleep had not been a problem for me, since Maude had breast fed, or at least I think she did since she always seemed to be fumbling with buttons on her frock and I never saw any bottles in the kitchen.

I went on the say that in my opinion, breastfeeding was best for baby, since the child wouldn't get confused by more than one person providing the food.

I added that this method of feeding also fitted well with their environmental beliefs since it combats global warming on the basis that they would not be using electricity to boil the kettle or power a bottle warmer. Also, there were the financial savings to be made through not having to buy formula milk, plus, in our case, important health & safety wins in not getting the milk powder stuff mixed up with my boxes of wood filler.

However, I added that whether they opted for breast or bottle, one thing was for sure, the child would throw as much back up as it swallowed. Some projectile vomit can make your muscles ache from constantly holding the child at arm's length to avoid getting a deluge of clotted cream in the chops, others were 'dribblers and would let go a silent stream of the stuff while they were held over your shoulder being winded.

Yet others let go in short, sharp bursts at the same time that they burped. This sort of vomit was the most challenging to deal with since there was no warning when it might happen, and when it did, the results could be shocking and dangerous to one's own appetite since my second son had a habit of doing this when I yawned, forcing me to share his meal and putting me off my favourite meal of chips and fried egg with onion gravy.

On the plus side, of course, I told them that once they knew the puking habits of their child, they could use this important intelligence to deal with any visitors they didn't like (and that there would be many such morons over the first few weeks of the child's life) by encouraging them to handle the child after feeding.

The chances are that the puke would send them packing.

I turned my attention to Robert and cautioned that, as the man of the house, this strange new little bundle of crap and wind would be the source of him, perhaps for the first time, being made to do all manner of domestic duties so that 'baby is comfortable'.

This might include being made to use the washing machine *and* hang the clothes out. I tell you, Reg, it took me weeks to get the handle of that hanger thing that looks like an upside-down umbrella.

I caught the thick end of Maude's tongue on more than one occasion when it folded back up under the weight of all those bloody nappies, which meant they had to be re-washed, which meant more smells like boiled cabbage coming from the kitchen.

While talking about boiled cabbage I again emphasised the choice they had in the nappy stakes and said that with so called disposable nappies you can chuck them in the bin: which in my view, would provide payback time in high summer for the council moving to fortnightly delivery, since their waste operatives were specially trained to lift the lid of wheelie-bins to check that no environmental criminals had dared place prohibited items like the council's newsletter, printed on100% recycled paper courtesy of a ton and a half of bleach and enough spin to dry a herd of water buffalo. I re-emphasised that the traditional nappy route may fit their environmental beliefs better and it would also improve Robert's engineering skills in the following ways…

a)   Such nappies needed sluicing down the kitchen sink then boiling for hours in a tin bucket on the gas stove. This produced that distinctive odour that told the neighbours not to visit and did wonders for weight loss since it put you off your tea. It also meant that from time to time, Robert would be called upon to demonstrate his skill with the rubber sink plunger to remove child waste solids and so unblock the sink ready for use in washing the salad for tea.

b)   It would assist in the proper division of labour since Jane would spend a considerable amount of time burning the enamelled tin buckets in which their little bundle of joy's nappies were boiled within an inch of their lives, while Robert would rapidly develop his metal bashing skills as he repaired said buckets.

For my part, Maude always complimented me on the quality of my rivets, and that I was the definition of what men stood for as I popped the rivets while wearing a gas mask and gauntlets sealed with rubber bands at the wrist. I have to say that it was good to know that my inventiveness was appreciated – and it also gave me precious time out of the house and in the shed with my beloved tools.

Noticing the concerned look on the newlyweds' faces, I quickly reassured them that nappies were but a passing phase and that the child would soon outgrow the ability of the things to handle the volume and weight of waste products to be contained. Not least because they would soon want to dress their beloved child in the latest fashion, which generally did not go well with a thick bundle of almost absorbent paper, or cotton equivalent hanging out of the leg holes.

In Maude's case it was khaki shorts. I think the material came from her father's Desert Rat Army uniform, Reg, which was the only thing he left when he ran off with that Iris Sitwell.

The mother-in-law always said that she wasn't surprised in the least when his little adventure ended badly, since Iris Sitwell had sat rather too well on the laps of Allied troops stationed in the village in preparation for D-Day, and the offspring he thought was the result of their 'funny doings', as the mother-in-law always put it, didn't exactly share his flaming red hair and jaundiced complexion.

At any rate, Maude's mother chucked her errant husband out when he tried to explain his 'little mistake' by saying he'd only gone to the shops for an ounce of old shag and he had been waylaid by Iris who spun him a tale about needing to get to the hospital to visit her dying dad.

And, that after 'commandeering' a motorbike from outside the tripe shop, he had no memory of the intervening 6 months and put it down to post-traumatic stress of his desert campaign.

When Maude's mother pointed out that Iris Sitwell wouldn't have known her father if she tripped over him in the street while holding his picture, and that her husband had spent his 'desert campaign' peeling spuds in the regiment's cookhouse, he knew the game was up and was last seen running from Iris Sitwell, who was throwing clothes pegs at him made out of army surplus shell casings, and screaming something about him being crap in bed and not holding a candle to 'her Rufus'.

Not long after, she followed 'Rufus' back to America with little Daisy in tow when his regiment was repatriated.

Anyway… continuing my instruction to the eager couple sat in front of me, I said that having grown, or crapped its way out of nappies, the child would enter the 'potty training' phase. And that this was not for the fainthearted. I added that they would soon position little moulded plastic containers that looked like an inside out version of a bicycle helmet at strategic locations around the house.

In the case of my eldest son, the stupid boy had a fetish for wearing them as a hat, whether empty or not.

I added that this was a dangerous phase as far as the health of the carpets are concerned, since that in order to encourage our own offspring to use the erstwhile bicycle helmet for its proper purpose, i.e. crap, Maude took the decision that the boy should be allowed to scamper around nappyless and without a pair of khaki shorts insight, on the grounds that at the first signs that the child needed to evacuate his overactive bowels (something he still suffers from I might add when he has been out for a curry), she could whisk him onto the nearest bicycle helmet.

The newlyweds then asked me what I meant by 'the signs'. I said that this was, to some extent, a mystery to me, also. Maude swore she could recognise such signs. Not only that, she could tell whether the child's efforts would lead to the production of either liquids or solids.

She maintained that a shiver meant liquids, and that purple cheeks and bulging eyeballs meant solids. I have to say that in the main this proved to be accurate. There are of course exceptions to every rule.

For example, when, on the several occasions the boy succumbed to a certain looseness of stool, it wasn't possible to read his face in advance. Instead, his surprised facial expression and bandy-leggedness heralded the ability to trace his exact movements around the house by no more than his movements if you take my meaning.

I counselled that as the child developed, things would change rapidly and all such changes would be easily observable by loving and attentive, if exhausted, parents, as they were sure to be. For example, having encouraged the child to start speaking during its first 12 months of life (or 15 months if a boy; lazy prats), they would spend the next 12 years telling it to be quiet, then a further 4 years wondering if it had lost its voice, save the ability to grunt, then the rest of its life wondering why any new sentence usually began with the words "Can I borrow…"

I then retraced my steps, joking with the newlyweds that I was getting ahead of myself and that before their life began to revolve around telling much loved offspring to shut up, the child would first take them through the interesting stage of hiding or removing anything of intrinsic or emotional value from within 3 feet of the ground as their little cherub learned to walk.

Of course, before managing to become fully vertical in a sustained and unaided manner, the little one would exhibit one or more forms of crawling, including:

a)   The bum shuffle: Efficient but expensive on trousers or leggings and can leave distasteful and hard to remove skid marks on carpets if a nappy fail occurs.

b)   The roly-poly: Early practice for rolling down grass banks when young; then into gutters as a drunken teenager and not suited for watching by anyone prone to the ill effects of vertigo or the sight of vomit.

c)   The back crawl: One for the confused child who thinks they're in a swimming pool. Tends to rub the hair from the back of the child's head leading to unsightly bald patches and parental worries about alopecia.

d)   The rocking horse: Highlighted by the child's tendency to rest on all fours in the manner of an animal, while moving backwards and forward on alternate strokes. Can be an early indicator of indecision and, if a boy, a worrisome tendency toward an unhealthy love of hillside dwelling animals. If a girl, an early indicator of the propensity to dress up as a hillside dwelling animal in order to attract the attention of boys with said predilection for hillside dwelling animals.

I added that once the child had mastered both crawling and shortly thereafter walking, their parental lower limbs would soon heal from the many lacerations caused by the child gripping onto their legs with a feline like tenacity as it shinnied its way up the loving parent in order to get to its feet, then latch onto its mother or father's kneecap with a gummy suck with more force than a limpet on the Great Barrier Reef.

They would also eventually recover from the financial implications of having to change home contents insurer on the basis that they had exhausted the number of allowable claims for china vases, plasma TVs and laptops to such an extent that the insurer would be prepared to pay them to find another provider.

I counselled that as a child progressed he or she would adopt one word and repeat it time and time again until it got its way, or until one or both parents ran from the room in tears swearing to get a goldfish next time.

I went on to tell them that one of the most powerful words the child would pick up from its parents and throw it back at them was 'no'. I therefore advised that when telling the child not to do something, or that it couldn't have whatever the object of its immediate craving was, they should be innovative in the word or words used.

For example, instead of saying 'no' when the child is about to pull the tablecloth off for the fifteenth time, the parent should say 'desist' or 'cease that', since these sorts of words are very difficult for small children to get their tongues around, especially considering that for some time, they will have only a couple of teeth and two attempts at the 's' word is to risk lacerating the underside of the tongue on its newly acquired tooth – which is something it will only do once, or at most twice before the child decides that the fun sound of breaking crockery, silent whimpering of its mother, and cries of 'it was your bloody idea to have a child' from its father, isn't worth the pain of a lacerated tongue or the strange sensation of blood swilling around its chops.

I added that while on the subject of chops, the other thing that they will notice is that the time will come, sooner rather than later, that their loving offspring wants to eat everything they are eating.

While I acknowledged that this can be quite amusing at first, I cautioned that the novelty would soon wear off when the child ended up eating more of the father's meal than the father enjoyed.

I found that the best way to deal with the situation was to strategically place a chip, sausage, fried bread or whatever healthy option their parents were enjoying, just out of reach of the child and while he or she was occupied as evidenced by going cross eyed and slobbering while pulling its arm joint out of its socket in trying to reach said healthy food.

At this point the mother can take full advantage of the child's open mouth to stuff in a spoonful of whatever mush comes out of those little bottles of baby food. This tactic may inadvertently add to the child's development and prepare it for a career as a goalkeeper.

It was at that point, Reg, that Jane asked what I thought another excellent question. She quizzed me as to whether I had any tips on minimising expenditure since they realised that especially in the first couple of years, having children could be very expensive.

Now, while I didn't have the heart to put them straight in as much as the early years will turn out to be, relatively speaking, the most inexpensive period of parenthood, I did tell them to be cautious in buying presents for the child for at least it's first two seasons of goodwill on the basis that:

a)   The child won't have a clue it's Christmas anyway.

b)   It will have received the world's entire supply of cuddly toys from its grandparents, aunties and uncles etc.

c)   The child will never remember the stupid outfits it's made to dress up in. Such photographs will come in as a handy blackmail tool when the child becomes a teenager and won't comply with instructions, since they will not want to look stupid in front of their peers. Parents should not underestimate how incredibly powerful this weapon can be.

However, I added that their ability to keep the full meaning of Christmas away from their beloved child; i.e. that it involves bankrupting their parents via the purchase of expensive rubbish that will be broken by the end of February, and at the same time that each of these wonderful gifts managed to find their way into the living room down the non-existent chimney from some invisible fat bloke in a red tunic who somehow managed to eat a plate of carrots and a box of mince pies – and that this was all the harder to explain to a wide-eyed young child by its father, when he was suffering from stomach cramps and diarrhoea.

Sensing the young newlyweds were beginning to suffer from information overload, and friction burns on their fingertips from continuing to wipe away the stale bird crap that continued to fall from the dappled branches above our heads and onto the now frayed shoulder pads of their organic and GM free Russet not shower proof jackets, I said that I would skip over the next couple of phases of the child development, saving only to highlight in the merest detail what they could expect, before moving on to the more serious subject of long-term family planning.

And so, Reg, I quickly listed the following:

a)   The terrible twos: a period when the child refuses to cooperate on any level whatsoever and is an early preparation for the teenage years. I advised that parents should lock themselves into the bedroom with a supply of chocolate and a DVD of *Chitty Chitty Bang Bang*, the Directors Cut, featuring scenes of the child catcher that the censor insisted on being taken out. Thus, the child would be left to its own devices in whichever room it was busy wrecking, and would usually fall asleep out of exhaustion, boredom or as a strategy to recuperate pending its parent's reappearance.

b)   The tooth fairy: I suggested that they used as a bedtime story from a very early age the tale of the orthodontist fairies who had no need of teeth anymore, since they had discovered a magic technique of growing metal anchors in their mouths onto which plastic veneers were attached giving them a lifelong set of immaculate teeth that never fell out and didn't require maintenance of any sort. Hence the bottom had fallen out of the market for children's teeth in line with the market forces of supply and demand. This had rendered teeth worthless and surplus to demand and that the parent was doing the child a favour by disposing of its discarded gnashers without levying a charge.

c)   Birthday parties: I stressed that these could be expensive and quickly get out of hand if they allowed the modern trend of the child inviting the whole of its class to the celebration, and that further, such celebrations must take place at a venue where the price per head was more expensive than the last birthday party the child had attended. I suggested that in order to pre-empt such demands this was the one occasion where their environmental credentials could play to their advantage, insofar as any requests for a birthday party could be met by the suggestion that the day should be spent clearing out some dilapidated woodland, or overgrown canal basin. I added that in today's world of iPads, online games and eating anything that didn't require a knife and fork, their child's peer group would avoid such invitations like the plague, leaving Jane, Robert and offspring to enjoy a pleasant hamper of carrot juice, birdseed and tofu sandwiches after a hard morning's work counting the lesser spotted field moth on some abandoned motorway construction site on account of it being the mating season.

d)   The first day at school: I sympathised that, while this may be a traumatic experience for the parents, since they would have to come to terms with learning to talk to one another again, in adult language and without the presence of their beloved child to camouflage what might otherwise allow the cracks in the relationship to show, their child will be more than happy to move on to the teacher as its new focus of amusement and challenge in terms of reducing said adult to tears.

e)   Puberty: I said that by this stage in the child's life, it may have stopped communicating to its parents in any meaningful way, save demands for food or money in words of one syllable. My advice was that they should not be unduly concerned since this was perfectly natural, because from the child's point of view, its parents had been born parents and could not possibly understand the confused world in which it now lived. I further advised that, in the particular case of boys, parents should not incessantly ask the man-child to keep repeating itself on account of his voice constantly veering from falsetto to double bass, since this will only increase the boy's sense of superiority. Instead they should tell the boy to write his requests on a piece of paper. This will have the advantage of improving the boy's skills in English grammar, and allow valuable practice in expressing himself in words of more than one syllable.

f) The first Romance: I counselled that this could be a particularly difficult time for parents and that it brought out particularly hypocritical traits in the father, on the basis that if it is his son who is bringing a new girlfriend to the house, the father will congratulate himself on breeding a boy capable of attracting a potential mate. If, on the other hand, it is his daughter who is bringing a new boyfriend into the family home, the father will want to beat the spotty youth around the head as a pre-emptive strike not to touch his daughter, or in any other way hinder her career due to motherhood.

This, Reg, brought my words of wisdom for the newlyweds to a conclusion by speaking of that which can strike fear into the heart of many a man; 'the snip'.

I did so on the basis of Robert's responsibility for family planning after they had acquired the agreed number of children, and before the after-effects of some boozy night out in years to come led to the purchase of more disposable nappies, or a new tin bucket in preparation for what they will describe to friends as 'their little surprise'.

Knowing that the subject of a vasectomy can be a difficult one to discuss for many men, I rose from the bench, shook the bird crap from my sleeves and, as I surveyed the village green that stretched out before me, on which I noticed the mother-in-law busy pursuing the latest meter reading man who'd been stupid enough to bend forward to undertake the task while Maude's mother was at striking distance.

Standing a pace or two from the bench with my back to the newlyweds also gave them the privacy I thought they may need as I advised on this delicate subject. I decided my approach would be to tell them of my own experience by way of giving Robert, in particular, confidence to take the necessary steps, (even if these would be hesitant for a day or two after the operation) when the time came.

From my perspective it was an easy decision. We'd got all the children we wanted, and Maude had promised to teach me how to use the microwave so that I could eat when she had a strop on with me, if I agreed to get my loose ends tied off, as it were.

So, having discussed the matter with our local doctor, I was referred to the local hospital where I saw what turned out to be a junior doctor.

Having explained how the operation was to be carried out, he asked if I had any questions. As you can imagine, two concerns came to mind:

a)   Would the operation hurt?

b)   Would I be in pain afterwards?

As to the former, he said that there wouldn't be any pain at all (although how the hell he would know at his age was beyond me unless doctors go through some kind of hypnotic process of feeling the pain they inflict on the patients – now wouldn't that be medical progress) and said that I should think of it as being stung in each testicle by a wasp.

Now I don't know about you, Reg, but I've never been stung anywhere by a wasp, never mind letting one of the little buggers anywhere near my meat and two veg. As for pain after the operation, he asked if I played rugby. I said I thought this an odd question when talking about a vasectomy.

He replied that it wasn't really since the pain from the operation would be like being kicked in the nuts by an opposing player on the rugby field. I imagine you can guess by now that I was losing all sense of confidence in this callow youth who had the temerity to call himself a doctor – even if only one that was learning the trade.

Nevertheless, feeling Maude's death stare on the back of my neck, I took the pen offered by the pimply faced doctor and signed the consent form in as manly a way as I could sum up. As promised, when we got home Maude taught me how to use the microwave before telling me she had been upset by my statement to the doctor that I didn't really see the need for a vasectomy since the Queen only had two birthdays a year, but that I was keen for my wife to celebrate these events without the worry or expense of having to buy a new tin bucket.

Even though I said to Maude that the callow doctor had looked confused and clearly didn't understand what I was talking about, Maude said I was insensitive and told me that now I knew how to use the microwave I could test my new skills since there was a chicken ready meal in the fridge and she was off to the bingo.

If you ask me, Reg, it was particularly cruel of Maude to say that I was in any way insensitive since it was my nuts that were about to be stung by wasps, and then kicked by a rugby player in size twelve boots.

Anyway, at least my first chicken-ding meal turned out all right and Maude lost at the bingo, so all in all, not a bad night.

In any event, the day of my surgery duly arrived. I had decided that I would dress up in my best suit replete with matching shirt and tie and stride confidently into the waiting room in order to show all present that a little argument with a wasp was no deterrent to me. Presenting myself to the little window at reception, I announced in a confident voice…

"I'm here for Mr Chandler," which was the name of my surgeon. Although looking a little distracted from shouting after a man who was running out the room and telling him to come back as he didn't have his trousers on and it wouldn't take long anyway, she brushed me aside with a wave of a hand and told me to go through the open doors on the opposite side of the room.

This I duly did and as soon as I was through the doors, I realised I was standing at the nurse's station around which a number of staff were paying close attention to the matron as she gave out the orders of the day. Standing there with my little overnight bag and best suit, I have to say I did feel a little self-conscious.

My position wasn't helped when my nervous movement caught matron's eye and she stopped relaying orders to the nurses as she turned to look me up and down before asking who I was and what I wanted.

I repeated with as much bravado as I could muster what I'd said to the lady behind the glass panel in reception and was immediately dismissed with a much more authoritative hand wave and told to sit in reception and wait my turn. As I gathered up as much dignity as I could muster, I could feel the hot breath steaming out of the matron's tonsils as she bellowed at the receptionist as to why I had been allowed onto the ward.

The hapless receptionist said that I had told her I was a medical representative to see Dr Chandler. Surprised at the accusation, I said that I had said no such thing but that I was here to see Dr Chandler.

The matron gave both of us a withering look and even Maude turned away, feigning that she was not with me, as the matron said that I was no such thing and was simply here to, as she put it "have his bits taken away." I suspected that the matron had a part-time job at the local vets and was called in whenever anything needed castrating.

Anyway, just as I was recovering what was left of my dignity, the receptionist told me to go through to the ward as they were ready for me. I'm sure you can fully appreciate my reticence at going through those doors again and it took some persuading from the receptionist that the matron was now on her break and the ward really was ready for me.

Picture the scene, Reg. A day ward with eight beds and eight terrified men, pretending not to be terrified, each with a little bag nestled neatly on top of his bed, looking around wondering what was to happen next.

Well, it didn't take long to find out, and since my bed was nearest the nurse's station, I was the first one to discover my fate. In came a rather big boned nurse who told me to sit on the bed, then told me not to sit on the bed but take my shoes off, then sit on the bed, before pulling round those curtain things.

She looked deep into my eyes and asked if I knew what the operation entailed. Sensing my moment of hesitation, she turned the papier-mâché container I hadn't noticed she'd brought with her upside down and retrieved a pen from her breast pocket.

She then explained the grisly details and for good measure, drew a rather poor representation of my men's bits (and not at all to scale, let me tell you), suitably annotated, on the container and, with rather more enthusiasm than I would have liked, struck two heavy pen lines, tracing each one several times for greater impact, to indicate the locations that the surgeon would separate my tubes, if you get what I mean.

Asking if I had understood all that she had said I replied immediately that I had, on the basis that had I hesitated in the slightest, she'd have gone through the whole bloody thing again.

Satisfied that I understood, she now turned the container the right way up and took away the hand that had been holding its contents in place. I looked blankly at her as she handed me a disposable razor and sachet of talcum powder.

"It's for down there, me-dear, you know, time to give yourself a Brazilian. Now make sure you do a good job because Dr Chandler will be very cross if he blunts his scalpel on your short and curlies, do I make myself clear?"

I started to ask how much enough was, but didn't get the chance to finish my question, since the portly nurse was already halfway through the curtain saying when I was ready, to get undressed, put on the gown provided and jump into bed. So there I stood, Reg.

In my stocking feet without either trousers or underpants to protect me from the goings-on on the other side of that curtain. Disposable razor in one hand, while my meat and two veg were shrinking in a defensive mood and disappearing into my groin at a rate of knots.

Now I don't know about you but seeing as the only place I have experience of using a razor is across my chops; and knowing how delicate my little Jimmy and his two mates felt at the best of times, it was with some trepidation, not least due to the lack of a mirror or other suitably shiny surface, that I undertook the task in hand, or in one hand, anyway.

Just at that moment I would've given a king's ransom for a can of shaving cream as dry powder on sensitive skin being cut with a sort of sharp edge doesn't do it for me, Reg.

It was even more difficult to dangle over the cardboard container to catch my now surplus lower region hair follicles.

To be safe in not incurring the wrath of the surgeon, since he would be the one with the knife, and I would be the one lying flat on my back, I decided to shave the lot off, which worked well in the short term but I paid dearly for it over the following weeks as it grew back, leaving me thinking I had a hedgehog hibernating and having a bad dream in my boxer shorts.

After finishing with the razor and checking I hadn't carried out my own vasectomy, I reached for the gown the big boned nurse told me to put on. I soon realised that what she called the gown was actually an oversized paper towel, which was, in any case, left gaping at the back.

Even after I'd tied the cord tight enough to restrict the blood supply to my lower half, if ever there was an incentive to climb into the cover of a hospital it was at that precise moment.

A short while later and without warning, nurse big bones flung the curtain aside and said it was time to go. I couldn't help noticing, Reg, that both she and the toothless porter with her had sly grins across their faces that shouted, "we know something you don't."

As they wheeled me out of the ward I heard a voice of protest from the man behind the curtains in the bed opposite mine…

"You're not shoving that thing up my arse."

After hearing him give a little yelp, I concluded that his protests had failed and that perhaps my day was going a little better than I thought after all.

Now it's not that I'm a coward, Reg, but I considered that in order to stay calm, I should avert my eyes from everything going on around me and instead concentrate on the ceiling above me. While this gave me a touch of vertigo as I was being wheeled from the ward and into the operating table, it did, for the most part, work.

I admit that the surgeon and his assistant must have thought me a little odd in not looking at them when they were talking to me by way of saying hello.

However, I had no intention of observing them using needles and suchlike while they went about their business, or to be more accurate, my business.

What did catch him by surprise was that from the corner of my eye, I could see out the window and into the building opposite. It struck me that if I could see them, they could see me, and I wondered whether the hospital, in order to raise more money, might not sell tickets in the way that airports used to sell you a day pass to the terminal roof so that you might watch the comings and goings of planes all day long.

After all, anyone watching my operation from across the quadrangle of the hospital wouldn't know who I was, unless they were allowed to use binoculars, which I would be against on principle, and I certainly wouldn't know who they were.

So that tells you what state of mind I was in as the two medical practitioners stood opposite one another at the foot of the operating table, blithely going on about what they were doing over the weekend, despite me wanting to scream at them that they should concentrate on what they were holding in their hands, which on this occasion, was me.

As I waited for the operation to begin, I scoured the crazed pattern on the ceiling tiles to see whether there were any wasps about, since I knew what was about to happen. Sure enough, as I strained my eyes to catch sight of the little blighters, two of them got me in the nuts.

Now I want to be supportive of the medical profession and I understand for reasons of political correctness why they are now not allowed to tell you to expect a 'little prick' when using a hypodermic needle.

However, from a trading standards point of view I take great exception to being told to expect a little scratch. Having a sharp metal tube, no matter how tiny, jabbed into your testicles can in no way be described as 'a little scratch'.

Nevertheless, medical practitioners are canny sods since they pinch, slap or in some other way accost another part of your body at the point of jabbing your nuts with a not-so-little prick in order to confuse your senses.

However, I was having none of it and let out a manly cough at the point of impact and began to retract my knees in an automatic response to being punctured.

To his credit the surgeon, for the most part, kept his temper and advised me not to move on the basis that if I did so again, I would be getting a sex change operation free of charge and there would be no need to take a specimen of any sort to the clinic in a month's time.

I thought honest advice and decided to relax my knees into a resting position. It was only at this point that I realised my nether regions were completely covered with a green sheet, save for a circular hole in the covering which, I assumed, gave access to my little fella and his two frightened friends. In my stupor and surprise at how painful a wasp sting to the nuts can in fact feel, I had a moment of panic and thought about the sex change he mentioned and were they delivering me of a child all in one fell swoop before the calming voice of the surgeon advised that from now on I wouldn't feel a thing.

Save for a peculiar feeling of liquid trickling down the inside of my thighs, on which I do not wish to dwell, he was telling the truth and within a few minutes, I felt the pull of stitches being completed before he patted me on the leg and said they were finished, before immediately turning back to his associate and debating the likelihood of its remaining dry over the weekend as he was off to a shooting party.

By now I was quite interested in the conversation but before I found out on whose estate he would spend his time obliterating anything that moved, the porter with the sick grin re-entered the room and wheeled me back to the ward.

With the deftest of touches, the big boned nurse pulled the curtains back around my bed and asked how I was feeling. Not waiting for me to respond she inspected the surgeon's stitches before announcing that he had done his usual neat job, then asked if I had remembered to bring a pair of tight underpants for extra support.

When I confirmed I had done so she told me to get out of bed and stand as straight as I could, which I managed with only the slightest of stoops. She then ordered me to lift one leg off the floor, then the other and as I concentrated on remaining upright, she pulled the underpants up as far as they would go, then lifted them another two inches for good luck causing me to wince and let out a throaty cough in a disguised a way as I could manage.

Ten minutes later, Maude was leading me out of the hospital and I was cursing how far it was to the car park since all the words of comfort I had heard from other men having undergone this 'little' operation turned out to be lies. While it didn't hurt, since my groin was still numb from the anaesthetic, it felt as though my nuts weighed a ton and I had the most peculiar sensation of knowing my legs were moving, but not necessarily attached to my hips.

The other lie that men tell is that it will be possible to return to work the following day without hindrance or discomfort.

I had to advise Robert that having been stung, then kicked in the meat and two veg, there was no way he wasn't going to feel the effect for a day or two.

My sage advice to the newlywed was that when the time came, to take the day after off, and instead lay quietly on the sofa with his legs slightly apart, and on no account allow the children near him, since they will instinctively know he is more sensitive than usual and will immediately seek to use his groin as a trampoline.

Nevertheless, I added that he will soon recover and before he knew, it would be time to take his sample to the clinic to check whether he was now firing blanks, so to speak.

In my own case, I was told to take my sample to the clinic in a little bottle a month later.

When I saw the doctor and produced the sample, she first of all showed great concern and said that she had never see a specimen of sputum like mine.

After saying it wasn't sputum, she threatened to call the police and told me I was a pervert before telling me to wash my hands and go around the corner to the family planning clinic. I swear, Reg, that the health service swap clinic locations around like supermarkets change their layout, just to confuse customers.

Anyway, once I had proved I had washed my hands and she had dowsed them in carbolic fluid, she said that she wouldn't call the police as long as I left the building by the time she put the carbolic fluid back in the cupboard.

Thankfully my nuts had returned to their normal size and I no longer felt as though I'd been in a horse saddle for six weeks, and so was able to comply with her request.

Do you know what, Reg, after I had finished telling Robert about my vasectomy a very touching thing happened. I turned around to see that the newlyweds were no longer on the bench. Instead, I traced the line of bird crap that led from where they had been seated and observed that they were walking across the village green with their arms around one another, offering each other a tissue – a touching sight, I thought, and my advice session had been a job well done.

END

About the Author

Phil Kingsman is a Brit and lives in the beautiful County of Norfolk, UK. His writing is largely based on his own life experiences, plus an overactive imagination.

In writing *The Crabby Old Git* series of short stories, Phil uses his crackers sense of humour to celebrate the tendency of many to offer advice to others, whether asked for or not, and the eccentricity some, and especially those (like him) of advancing years who, as he puts it "Have hair growing from places they didn't have places 20 years ago."

Printed in Great Britain
by Amazon